# Mythic Delirium

# Also by Mike Allen

*Novels*

The Black Fire Concerto

The Ghoulmaker's Aria (forthcoming)

*Short Fiction Collections*

Unseaming

*Poetry Collections*

Hungry Constellations

The Journey to Kailash

Strange Wisdoms of the Dead

Disturbing Muses

Petting the Time Shark

Defacing the Moon

*As Editor*

Clockwork Phoenix 4

Clockwork Phoenix 3:
New Tales of Beauty and Strangeness

Clockwork Phoenix 2:
More Tales of Beauty and Strangeness

Clockwork Phoenix:
Tales of Beauty and Strangeness

Mythic 2

Mythic

The Alchemy of Stars:
Rhysling Award Winners Showcase (with Roger Dutcher)

New Dominions:
Fantasy Stories by Virginia Writers

Edited by Mike and Anita Allen

Mythic Delirium
BOOKS

mythicdelirium.com

Mythic Delirium



Mythic Delirium logo design by Tim Mullins

ISBN-10: 0988912430
ISBN-13: 978-0-9889124-3-4

Published by Mythic Delirium Books
mythicdelirium.com

Further copyright information begins on page 170.

Our gratitude goes out to the following who because of their generosity are from now on designated as supporters of Mythic Delirium Books: Saira Ali, Cora Anderson, Anonymous, Patricia M. Cryan, Steve Dempsey, Oz Drummond, Patrick Dugan, Matthew Farrer, C. R. Fowler, Mary J. Lewis, Paul T. Muse, Jr., Shyam Nunley, Finny Pendragon, Kenneth Schneyer, and Delia Sherman.

*To all of you chasing*
*your own writing dreams:*
*never give up.*

# Contents

# Myths and Delusions: An Introduction

## *Mike Allen*

There's a long, odd story behind the making of this book—and if you're not the sensible kind who skips straightaway to the poems and stories, then I'm happy to share it.

*Mythic Delirium* began with a whim, a fitting start for a project with such a name. At first it was nothing more than a fanciful logo I drew during my undergraduate years, back before the era of cellphones and email.

Creative college kids make all kinds of plans they never follow through on. Some friends and I batted about an idea for a magazine, thought *Mythic Delirium* would be a cool name for it. I never seriously thought about becoming a publisher, had not the slightest understanding of what that would entail.

Skip forward three years to 1995, four-year college and grad school both behind me, the future clear as a mist full of hungry ghosts. A fellow who I believed to be another journeyman writer, standing a rung or two higher than me on the ladder, told me he'd fund an anthology of local writers if I'd edit it. Once I had the book together, I discovered he was a pathological liar who'd never published a thing in his life.

I went forward with the book, using my own money, a commodity in short supply. And *New Dominions: Fantasy Stories by Virginia Writers* was, on a handmade, small-press scale, a smash success. There were sales! There was newspaper coverage! There were reviews! There were doors that opened for me in the field of speculative fiction! Not to mention, I had helped bring retired pulp writer Nelson S. Bond back into the limelight. And most all of the writers I published in that odd little book, including Nelson, became friends I still treasure.

I still knew nothing about publishing. Yet somehow I'd succeeded at it anyway, so there was no turning back.

Fast-forward three more years. I'd been a part of *Event Horizon*, one of the earliest webzines—no, not the one helmed by Ellen Datlow, though those folks paid us a moderate sum so they could have exclusive rights to the name. Certain that editing and publishing were going to be part of my bag of tricks from then on, but unsatisfied with less-than-reliable partnerships, I decided to set out on my own. I'd never forgotten that name I brainstormed all those years ago.

And so I launched *Mythic Delirium*.

Money was still scarce, and I had no intention of abandoning my writing ambitions, so I scaled the project to something I thought I could handle. I would publish twice a year. I would only publish poetry, and formal poetry at that. I created the zine's first cover, crudely assembled using a bootleg photo manipulation program, printed on my inkjet. I could barely afford the ink cartridges, so I printed as many issues as I could in one go, and when the ink ran out (astonishingly quickly!) returned them as defective and got replacements.

I produced two issues. Only a handful subscribed. Submissions were sparse. Reviewers, temperamentally opposed to the idea of a zine recovering its expenses, said I charged too much for too little content. Warren Lapine of DNA Publications moved to Virginia, and I started reading slush for his hard sci-fi magazine *Absolute Magnitude*. I decided that would fill out my editing resume nicely, and quietly retired *Mythic Delirium* to the land of limbo.

Then, in the pages of *The Year's Best Fantasy and Horror*, Ellen Datlow included my defunct zine in her list of best magazines of the year. Warren saw that, and asked me to revive it for DNA. I hemmed and hawed at first, but then realized this was a chance I couldn't let drop.

So *Mythic Delirium* relaunched as a sister magazine to *Absolute Magnitude*, *Aboriginal SF*, *Weird Tales* and *Science Fiction Chronicle*. I lifted the restrictions on form, and the modest pay rates Warren agreed to fund still provided me with a budget beyond anything I could have swung on my own. The presence of writers like Jane Yolen from our third issue forward drew submissions from the likes of Sonya Taaffe (we were the first to publish her poetry) and Theodora Goss (who wrote the first poem in our pages to win a Rhysling Award.)

I'm certain *Mythic Delirium* was the only magazine devoted exclusively to poetry in the history of speculative literature to have the backing of a publisher that size. I was able to seek subscriptions through mass mailings, and Warren had my back financially when I approached Ursula K. Le Guin for a special two-issue project.

And yet.

There came a time when I could no longer deny that the DNA ship was sinking and I couldn't stay on board if I wanted *Mythic Delirium* to live.

But it wasn't as hard as it could have been. Even under DNA, *Mythic Delirium* remained essentially a DIY-zine. Our cover artist, Tim Mullins, printed the covers himself, using better means that I had at my disposal. By this time I worked at a newspaper rather than a department store warehouse, and I could afford to print the rest of the zine myself. Anita and I would collate the pages with the covers and bring them to a copy shop for binding. The results were just professional enough. But still . . . I had to cut the zine's already meager pay rates to keep it going. I had no idea whether the speculative community would keep supporting *Mythic Delirium* without the might of DNA behind it.

As it turned out, the community had our backs.

*Mythic Delirium* supported itself for four years after DNA and I parted ways, and just when it looked like it might finally run aground, Neil Gaiman at last followed up on a longstanding request and offered us an original poem, one inspired by his wife-to-be Amanda Palmer, just in time for our 10th anniversary issue in 2009.

Once again, a windfall brought us to the attention of a whole new audience.

Fast-forward four more years.

We weren't bad to start with, but we'd been getting better and better and better at what we did. Poems like Amal El-Mohtar's "Song for an Ancient City" and Catherynne M. Valente's "The Melancholy of Mechagirl" and many others will ensure *Mythic Delirium* has a lasting legacy. And yet we're now in an age when the Internet rules, when print destabilizes more each year, and even a tiny zine like ours can't dodge the winds of change.

*Mythic Delirium* had stopped paying for itself. Its reserves were slowly dwindling.

And at the same time, I was itching for a change. I wanted to join the revolution.

By this time, I'd experimented with hybrid poetry and prose anthologies (*MYTHIC* and *MYTHIC 2*, both 2006) and proven my chops as a fiction editor with the first three *Clockwork Phoenix* anthologies. And much like I had with *Mythic Delirium*, I had taken over responsibility for *Clockwork Phoenix* from a failing publisher and revived it on my own, with help from the speculative fiction community, and from Kickstarter. I asked for $5,000 to put together *Clockwork Phoenix 4*, and backers stepped up to give Anita and me more than $10,000.

Kickstarter reverses the standard small-press paradigm. Rather than risking all your own money on a project with limited prospects—however worthwhile it may be from an artistic point of view—the entire project arrives with every cost covered and every copy pre-sold. It's up to you, the creator, to make sure the expenses match the revenue.

And well, if you can do it, it's a godsend. It sure was for us. I'll be thanking our Kickstarter backers for the rest of my life.

Not least for this: our final stretch goal for the campaign sought seed money to start a new webzine—and we made it. I was preparing, in a way, to come full circle.

I decided it was time for *Mythic Delirium* to transmogrify. To stop being a dinosaur and join the digital age.

Rose Lemberg, an amazing editor and writer herself, and a fan of the *MYTHIC* books, suggested the model. The zine would keep its poetry leanings, far heavier than verse-timid genre zines are willing to lift, and introduce fiction to the mix.

But Anita didn't want *Mythic Delirium* to abandon print altogether, and neither did I.

So we held our second Kickstarter, the one that functioned as a subscription drive, to fund the new *Mythic Delirium* past its first year. Our supporters came through with flying colors: we asked for $2,500 and raised $3,500.

Our stretch goal for our second Kickstarter reversed the first: where the first stretched book funding to finance a digital zine, the second stretched the digital zine's funding to finance a book.

Fast-forward to the book you are now holding in your hands.

And at last, a few words about the content.

First, we didn't want this to be just a straight repeat of Issues 0.1 through 0.4 of *Mythic Delirium* Mark II.

For all the *Clockwork Phoenix* volumes and for many of the issues of *Mythic Delirium* Mark I, Anita took the stories and poems and arranged them in orders that connected and highlighted themes, that made them flow as a whole. She's done that here, providing these works with new contexts and presentations. This is not just an omnibus, but a full-blown anthology. We hope you enjoy the directions the currents veer.

Second, in imagining what sort of thing we publish, people tend to concentrate on the "Mythic" in our title . . . and forget the "Delirium." But we give equal emphasis to both. My ideal for the new *Mythic Delirium* is a publication that makes our notoriously offbeat *Clockwork Phoenix* seem like a product of the straight and narrow. Perhaps we're not there yet, but I think you'll agree that what's taking shape is strange indeed.

Third, in addition to Anita, two other key personnel have to be thanked for their vital roles in the magazine's new life: Francesca Forrest, intrepid copy editor for both the Mark I and Mark II incarnations, and Elizabeth Campbell of Antimatter Press, who actually orchestrated the digital part of our digital transformation.

Finally, I'd be remiss if I didn't point out that *Mythic Delirium* neither begins nor ends with what you'll find here. To explore our previous incarnation, and to sample the stories and poems we've published since these works first appeared, join us at mythicdelirium.com once you've finished here.

If there's one lesson we've learned from all of this, it's that a good show goes on.

—Roanoke, Va., June 2014

# This Talk of Poems

*Amal El-Mohtar*

I will tell you this thing,
as I do
(this is the game we play together:
one retracts the half-revealed,
one coaxes out what's left concealed). This, then,
is what I will say to you,
stumbling over your eyes' architecture,
a clumsy grasping after words—
I called your eyes cathedrals, was sincere,
and blush to remember how you laughed—
this, then, is what I will say—

no, I can't. Not yet! Not now,
not when the secret curls and stammers
while you clamour insistence, disbelief—not now,
but later, perhaps, when you don't expect
a sudden surge of metaphor,
a tidal rush, a rising line of foam and salt
to soak shock into your ankles.

We're not there yet. Not yet at the place
where I can tell you how I think
of days when you'll tell some other girl
about this girl who read you poems
thinking you enjoyed them, thinking
you listened to anything more than the sound of her voice,
the funny lilting of her foreign vowels
and her foreign cadence,
mixing syllables and emphases
while longing for yours.

"She even wrote me a poem," you'll say,
to this other girl, cool and secure
in her place at the end of your history,
"and it was a bit shit, but what do I know
about poetry."

I won't tell you this, won't read you this,
because how could it ever be the time
to tell you I write in self-defence,
to tell you that to write to you
is to think of you hurting me—
to imagine you hurting me
if you haven't yet—

and to remember that when I said
*those poems I wrote for other people*
*those poems I didn't write for you*
*are full of thorns, are healing stings,*
*are scabbing over wounds*—
you said,
*you don't care about me enough*
*to write a poem*—
but meant
*you don't care about me enough*
*to let me hurt you.*

You'll say this isn't fair. How could you know
that a poem is a grudge
clutched tight against the liver, bile-steeped,
nursed to savage potency? How could you know
that a poem is catharsis,
is septic in conception, a boil
lanced in execution?

You never listened, after all,
to anything but the sound of my voice.

So I'll cut you this slack. Here is a poem.
It isn't pretty, it isn't built

of honey and spice, isn't sweet
or savoury, isn't anything
like what a poem is thought to be.
I won't call you Green Man, Diamond Jack,
Knight of Coins or Pentacles,
won't speak of stretching out on graves,
or how the tracery of your irises
might have taught architects to dream
of stained glass.

I certainly won't tell you I love you.

And maybe once you've read it,
to yourself, in quiet,
in your own mind's voice,
you'll think twice before asking me
to write you another.

# The Wives of Paris

## *Marie Brennan*

They offered him a beautiful woman, power over men, victory in war.

So of course he chose the beautiful woman. He was a young man, after all. Power would come—don't forget, he was the son of a king—and victory was guaranteed, because all young men are invincible . . . but a woman's soft thighs are another matter. To a teenager, that is the fruit of Tantalus: only divine intervention can bring it within reach.

Aphrodite cleared up his acne, taught him how to flirt, and sent him off to Sparta. And the rest is well-known myth.

NEVER MIND OENONE. (No one ever does.) Menelaus, sure, people remember him; how many guys start a war over a simple case of adultery? Nobody remembers the nymph Paris abandoned. Even though she did the Morgan le Fay thing, and sent her son—Paris' son—to try and betray Troy to the Greeks. Even though she did the Hallgerðr thing, and refused Paris the assistance that might have saved his life. Even though she did the thing done by women in tales the world over, and committed suicide after he was dead.

Oenone, *Οἰνώνη*, nymph of wine. Maybe she was drunk when she met Paris. She wouldn't be the first woman to make that mistake, seeing a young man, *knowing* he's going to break her heart, and giving it to him anyway. Sure, she had more than just instinct to warn her; she had *prophecy*. But who ever pays attention to that?

SAY PARIS WAS different. Still seventeen years old, still exiled from Troy to herd sheep on Mount Ida, but with more on his mind than just sex. After all, he's married to a nymph, and we all know what *they're* like, the little tarts. He's already getting enough action.

A beautiful woman, power over men, victory in war. He's never seen war, but power sounds nice. More interesting than this hillside, anyway. Especially when Hera dangles the extra incentive of gold, jewels, riches beyond his (rather limited) imagination. Oenone never seems to care that she's married beneath herself, that he's a sheep-herder and she's an immortal nymph, but it bugs him.

So he tells Aphrodite her ass is too fat for his taste, and hands the golden apple to Hera. Hey presto, power.

It takes a little longer than that, of course. She isn't a genie, to conjure up a kingdom for Paris out of thin air, and bumping off his dad (not to mention his forty-nine brothers) to make him King of Troy seems rather in poor taste. But marriage, that's a respectable road to both power and riches.

Enter Lamia. (Hera can see the future, too. Leave any woman unattended for long enough, and Zeus will try to sleep with her; it seems kinder to make sure Lamia is attended than to get vengeance later by making her eat her own children.) She's a queen of Libya, and as she hasn't yet ripped out her own eyes over the kids-for-dinner thing, she's passably pretty. No Helen, but then again who is, and since Paris has never laid eyes on Helen, it doesn't much matter. This is a political match anyway, made for the purpose of world domination.

She's always wanted to take over Egypt. Not with an army; armies are unsubtle things, and Lamia has a serpent's subtlety. Instead she and her new husband offer a trade-pact here, a treaty there, a marriage of some Egyptian daughter to a Libyan son. (Paris acknowledges the boy as his own, and that's enough for political purposes, even though the kid's skin is black as coal.) Pretty soon various Greek cities are client-states to the North African empire. Their caravans and ships venture from the Pillars of Hercules to the far reaches of the East, bringing back spices and emeralds and letters of friendship from foreign potentates.

Nobody besieges the gates of Troy. Why should they? It's a backwater, a forgotten little city, neglected by the great power that now rules half the known world and has alliances with the other half. Paris hasn't forgotten that his father dumped him on Mount Ida to herd sheep. Old Priam lives long enough to see his kingdom wither, starved for trade, its young people migrating to greener pastures. Twenty-three of Paris' brothers end up working for the Libyan court, in one minor clerical position or another. Not Hector, of course; it's beneath a crown prince's dignity. He puts together a force of warriors instead, intending to attack whatever target presents itself. They never make it out the door: Priam keels over of a very convenient heart attack, so everything stops for the funeral games, and while that's going on Hector discovers Troy's in debt up to its eyeballs. Faced with a choice between selling himself in marriage to some foreign princess, and watching what remains of his kingdom be carved up among its neighbors, he falls on his sword.

Paris never hears about any of this. Lamia sees to it that his flunkies don't trouble him with such insignificant trifles.

Oenone's heart is broken, of course. Paris didn't abandon her on Mount Ida; he and Lamia agreed from the start that there's no reason to expect marital fidelity, so long as there are enough acknowledged children to marry off for alliances. But Oenone pines for their days of bucolic peace; at this remove, it's easy to forget the annoyance and toil that caring for sheep actually requires. She preferred the sheepherder to the king, anyway. She feels like she doesn't even know Paris anymore.

She goes to tell him this, and he stares blankly at her, like she's speaking—well, not Greek. Russian, maybe. Weeping, Oenone asks if he knows *her* anymore.

A flunky, ushering the devastated nymph out the door, explains that they don't trouble the king with such insignificant trifles as her name.

SO POWER CORRUPTS—but we knew that already. And thinking with the downstairs brain never ends well. What's behind door number three?

Up the aggression a bit, and you've got a Paris who dreams of glory on the battlefield. The daughter of Zeus is more cunning than her sisters, or whatever you call the wife of the guy whose head you sprang out of, and the chick born from the sea foam created by the genitals of a dead ur-god. (No doubt the Germans can build nouns for these things.) She doesn't dangle breasts or gold. She merely looks at him, and *looks* at him, until he squirms and reddens and decides he's got to prove something to the grey-eyed bitch. Victory in war, please, and you other two can shove off.

Athena makes him earn it—which means he has to learn something other than sheep—which means he needs a teacher. All the fashionable heroes go to Chiron, but she's bored with the centaur's style, and decides to try something new. She sends him to Penthesilea.

The Queen of the Amazons gives Paris plenty of reason to regret his choice. Her followers are less than pleased with having to train a man; they threaten to cut off his balls several times a week. (The threats are that often, not the cutting. Unlike Prometheus' liver, his balls would *not* grow back.) And the training itself is boot camp from hell, for a fellow whose most vigorous exercise until now has been sporting with a nymph. But Penthesilea is nothing if not determined, and after a while they both start to enjoy it, the discipline and the shouting matches and eventually the sex, which is nothing like it was with gentle Oenone.

Hercules. Theseus. Achilles. . . . and Paris. Menelaus wouldn't be able to kick *this* kid's ass, not once Penthesilea is done with him. The Amazons abandon her, muttering in disgust about that prick corrupting their queen, but the two of them hardly care; together Paris and his warrior-wife rampage around the Mediterranean, collecting an army of rabid followers and laying waste every kingdom and city-state you care to name, before returning to Troy in triumph. There Paris "suggests" to his aged father and forty-nine brothers that maybe it's time for a fresh rump on the throne. They're smart enough not to argue.

And when the debts of his rampage come due, nobody breaks a sweat. So what if every kingdom and city-state in the Mediterranean wants a piece of Troy's hide? Their king's got Athena on his side. She won't let him lose.

Not in war, anyway. But she promised him victory, not wisdom, and nobody planned for Oenone. Nor for the Amazons, who haven't forgotten that their queen waltzed off with some dick-swinging jerk. Jilted nymph plus psychotic warriors equals a plan that, while not as iconic as a giant wooden horse with Greeks inside, gets the job done.

One hundred harlots enter the city of Troy. Ninety-nine disperse through the soldiers' quarters, gritting their teeth into something like a smile. The hundredth makes her way up to the palace, where she pours poisoned wine down the throats of her erstwhile husband and the tramp he ran off with.

It doesn't take ten years. It doesn't even take ten hours. Half the soldiery is dead by morning, and the gates are jammed open; every Trojan with common sense grabs their portable wealth and flees.

What's left descends into chaos and looting, and when the armies finally show up, they burn what little remains.

STOP ME IF you've heard this one before. There's a kid, and you just *know* he's going to be trouble, so you decide to prevent it by offing him. Only you're too squeamish to actually do the deed, so instead you handle it in a roundabout way—abandoning him on a mountainside, say, where you can be deceived about the attempt's success.

It didn't work for the parents of Oedipus; it didn't work for the uncle of Romulus and Remus—hell, it didn't work for Snow White's step-mother—but why mess with tradition? Off to the mountainside with little baby Paris. As proof of his death, the herdsman presents a dog's tongue. And Priam and Hecuba sleep soundly, knowing they sent their son off to be murdered . . . but at least he won't be the ruin of his homeland, as the prophets had foretold.

Except he will, of course, because Fate's a bitch—three of them—and mountainsides never work like they're supposed to. You can't blame Helen: her face may have launched a thousand ships, but Paris is the one who brought them to Troy. He was always going to bring destruction. Athena and Hera couldn't change that. No woman, mortal or divine, could.

Nor even poor, forgotten Oenone. Paris' first wife, who knew he was going to break her heart, and gave it to him anyway. Get rid of the golden, discord-causing apple; get rid of the three goddesses who have nothing better to do with their time than squabble about who's the prettiest. Leave him there on Mount Ida, a simple shepherd with his nymphly wife.

He'll *still* find a way to bring it down.

But maybe there's happiness in that simplicity, before it falls apart. No politics; no bloodshed; no marriages broken by an adulterous spouse.

And no epic poetry, spanning the gulf of ages, singing of glorious tragedy.

Oenone would not complain.

# Cuneiform Toast

*Sonya Taaffe*

To the god of the backstairs,
the fixer, the cutter of fates
sharp-slit with the morning's mail,
his deskful of papers
chills and heartache,
headache, brain-fever, last breath,
the seizing storm that fastens on his victims
straightening his glasses, discreet with his handkerchief
from the quick run up the steps to heaven,
minister of the country none return from,
hell's messenger boy, so I always imagined you.
Remember me to your mother, wife, and daughter,
handing on these words like a cup of Siduri's beer,
initial the requisitions, file the weekly reports,
tell your mistress to forget my name.

# Hexagon

*Alexandra Seidel*

## 1 Recognition

Scheherazade feels heat blushing her cheeks but with the rain falling heavy and thick and the steel gray sky overhead, the color seems just background noise. She forgot her umbrella, and now she stands on the sidewalk, naked to the rain. All her clothes melt to her skin, and she feels like drowning. Across from her, she sees the man who makes everyone else turn into inconsequential extras, who is like a lighthouse banishing reef and rock from her mind. *Shahrayar*, she thinks, *I know you.*

Shahrayar turns, and he stops. They are each caught in the stillness of a snow globe, the world around them turmoil, but between them time stretched paper thin.

Scheherazade thinks of a night—just one single night—broken into a thousand pieces. She realizes her throat has been a knot for a long time, but now, it is finally free, unobstructed.

"Once upon a time, there was a girl who knew the name of all she saw from the moment she saw it . . ." she says, her words barely a whisper.

But Shahrayar hears her.

## 2 Premonition

Baba hums an ancient melody as she measures the flour, the sugar, as she breaks the eggs. Scheherazade is cleaning and peeling apples at the table, the girl's dark curls running down over her red sweater, a scarlet scarf around her throat. The scarf blends with the color of apple peels in the bowl in the girl's lap.

There has not been a day when Baba has known her grandchild to be that silent and without a tale to tell. The old woman's melody pushes to minors. *Not a day with this forlorn look on her face, not a day when she was here, but wasn't.*

"Once upon a time, there was a girl who would visit her grandmother each and every day, sheathed in a scarf that the grandmother had made for her, a scarf she had made *only* for her," Baba whispers, melody forgotten.

She takes another egg, cracks it, and lets the contents drop in the mixing bowl only to discover that it's all bloody inside. *The cake is ruined,* she thinks, her wrinkles deepening.

At the table, Scheherazade utters a short screech. The girl has cut herself with the kitchen knife, three drops falling from her finger and on the peeled white apples.

*Ruined,* Baba thinks.

## 3 Suspicion

Selene runs a hand over her belly, a habit already though it is still early. Shahrayar reads the paper across from her, but his eyes are not moving with the words. The mug of coffee in front of him has grown cold.

Inside her, something twists.

"Once upon a time, there was a girl, and all around her, there was glass," Selene whispers.

Her eyes on fire she rises, knocking over the cold coffee. The dark brown liquid spills over the table, over Shahrayar's white shirt, and she knows that it will stain. He has dropped the newspaper, stares at her wide-eyed as if he had forgotten she was even there to begin with.

"Look at me, Shahrayar!" she says, one hand on her belly. But his eyes are marbles of glass, as if a coffin lid had been shut over them.

Shahrayar no longer sees her, she realizes.

## 4 Rubicon

Behind the receptionist's desk, Binnoire is busy tuning her guitar. She used to play the harp once, but harps are so sad, and she has found that the sadness of a guitar is lighter, easier for her to bear.

The couple approaches her desk shyly, yet not uneager. The girl's hair and eyes are dark with the ink of generations of stories, and her skin vibrates bronze to match. The man is bearded, hair growing wild as if it were looking for the moon.

"Once upon a time, there was a girl who got lost in the woods, her ankles bitten by wolves, her eyes blinded by thorns from the enchantress's garden," Binnoire whispers.

She rents them a room for the hour, shrugs as they enter the elevator. *Nothing anyone can do*, she thinks and picks up her guitar again. Today, her fingers stain and ache as she coaxes a melody from the old strings that is dark and heavy and sad.

**5 Retrospection**

Vera's eyes know the truth already, but her mind struggles to catch up. It is the curse of younger siblings, always struggling to catch up. Scheherazade's lifeless body lies somewhere under that train. *Please let it be whole. Please please please.*

The other woman had approached them as they waited for the train. Her eyes had been an afrit's, hot and mad with anger, and she had held her belly wracked with cramps. While they waited, that afrit-eyed woman had ambushed them, demanded to talk to Zadie. *We'll just talk at the other end of the platform,* Zadie had said. *I'll be right back . . .*

"Once upon a time, there were two sisters, the one fair as snow, the other dark as pitch . . ." Vera whispers to herself as her mind catches up and the tears flow from her. The darkness and the screams come later.

**6 Observation**

Sepho never judges. The body on her table is that of a girl, blond hair like moonbeams. She was perhaps four months pregnant when she took the pills. Sepho can see it in the rounder forms, the softer edges of the hips and breasts. Cremation, the husband said. Quiet, the husband said, uncrying. Sepho knows of the murder of course, everybody knows, news of that kind travel so far and fast. The colleague who handled the other body, the body of the girl who was pushed, said there was nothing to be done, the damage too great. Eyes popped out, skull cracked, limps torn loose and scattered. Nothing to be done.

Sepho looks down at her charge. *Nothing to be done,* she thinks.

"Once upon a time, there were two sisters who thought they had fallen in love with a true prince," Sepho says quietly as she tries to straighten the body's hand that is angled strangely upward, as if to reach for the abdomen.

Sepho works quietly, precisely. There are so many stories, she often thinks to herself.

And Sepho knows the ending of them all.

# Unmasking

## *Sandi Leibowitz*

Never say you minded

Never say you didn't guess
        it was my quickening inside her
        that made verses fly from her lips
        like frosty breath up to the winter stars

Do not lie that you preferred
the pale girl hiding behind night-black hair
too shy to ask for kisses
        to sly me who never asked
        just took them

Foxes are thieves by nature;
I can't be blamed for stealing your heart

Never say that under
the gleaming egg of the full moon
        you did not spy my true self,
        glimpse eyes of golden smoke,
        fur red as sunset nuzzling autumn maples,
        hear the snap of fine sharp teeth
        each time I nipped your nape in play
Unmask yourself as well,
my three-season husband,
and confess:

        you'd readily exchange my snarls
        for her most precious compliments,
        my barks of joy for her submissive mews,

would sooner chase me through sweet-scented grass
than catch her in your kitchen

Kitsune are not keen on winter leavings
We crave love fresh,
still squirming like a live hen in the jaws
With the flick of nine snow-tipped tails
I leave you

I will not say
that I'll forget you

# Ahalya: Deliverance

## *Karthika Naïr*

**I. Glosa:** ***No More***

अब मुझे कोई इंतजार कहाँ
वोह् जो बहते थे आबशार कहाँ
आँख के एक गाव में, रात को ख़्वाब आते थे
छूने से बहते थे, बोले तो केहते थे
"उडते ख़्वाबों का ऐतबार कहाँ."

No more now do I have to wait.
No longer now, those cascades, do they rush.
In a hamlet of my eyes, dreams once dwelt at night.
If touched, they would flow; if asked, they would reply:
"There is no trusting volant dreams."

—Gulzar, Ab mujhe koi intezaar kahan (Ishqiya, 2010)
Translation by KN

No. No more. No more lies, no lapses. No more myths
sown on time from slivers of early monolith,
the mirror you call truth. Ballads sail down millennia,
hurl livid blooms—*kapala, shapita, kalankini.* . . .
wretched, accursed, adulteress—on my name, smithed
once from heaven's ore. Denigrate
me no more—or not yet: hear first, and firsthand, from women
like me, the tales *they* never sing—the myth-makers, the saints,
the gods. Stones, too, can rise in spate.
No more now do I have to wait.

For it is time. Time to rouse the skies, reinstate
Earth's archives, seek the seas' lost chants. They'll vindicate
virtue, speak in my stead, resound: I am she, Ahalya.
*Mahabhagha.* Mind-born to Brahma. Flawless. Free—free, like
thought was, and should be. Eternal. Inviolate.
The first maiden, forged, full-grown, in the hush
of nascent time; matter mixed and cast with planets, seasons,
stars. They said he'd minted dusk's flame for my lips; shaped rivers—
their flow, their tumble—from my tresses. (They're lush
no longer now, those cascades. Do they rush

out—pale, fraught—to drown underground? But I digress).
Yes, my father—architect of three worlds, no less—
had decked virgin moon with my glow, scattered the smells of spring
between my thighs, my breasts; smiled in naïve, paternal pride
then summoned gods, gandharvas, yogins, nymphs, "Witness
these new wonders." Like fruit flies to coloured delights
they gathered, buzzing in envy, awe, greed and lust. Desire
spread in nitid plague: some clamoured earth; one, thunder; one bid
for death. I'd be the big prize—not love to requite.
In a hamlet of my eyes, dreams once dwelt at night—

once. Now, this scene walks there, sleepless: Brahma, aghast,
skirting whirlpooling plaints, seeks shelter in the mast
of a seer's voice, 'Chattel she shan't be. No creature may claim
earth, air, heaven. Ahalya binds all three. Them I worship,
her I've guarded.' Thus does great Gautama, steadfast
scripter, win my hand: with words fluid and spry.
Thus do fathers belie their own premises; swap suffrage
for safety. In fear lies the key. But I, unafraid,
am not heard, nor asked, for desires are not coy.
If touched, they would flow; if asked they would reply:

'We are born to soar, not self-destroy.' Thus was I
wed—with sour gods to witness, dark rain to defy
the bond Agni alloyed—then sent, in fulgent wrapping, with
this aged, agelast, sudden spouse. Co-wives, their scions
and sacred books of cosmic law would await my
service: what else could, my sire deemed,

reflect my worth? 'No human should hope for more, devotion
will now be your awl. Amsa of my breath, forget the lore:
those pledges you cannot redeem.
There is no trusting volant dreams.'

## II. Glosa: *Until late have I stayed awake*

जागे हैं देर तक, हमें कुछ देर सोने दो
थोड़ी सी रात आर है,सुबह तो होने दो
आधे अधूरे ख़्वाब जो पूरे न हो सके
एक बार फरि से नीद में वो ख़्वाब बोने दो.

Until late have I stayed awake, let me sleep awhile.
A trace of the night remains; wait, let morning appear.
Those half-grown dreams that could not be fulfilled . . .
Let me sow, in my sleep, those dreams once more.

—Gulzar, Jaage hain der tak (Guru, 2007)
Translation by KN

Time was all things: tenebrous, tall, sometimes winged. Peat
were my days, growing piles of wet, spent earth replete
with husks of dead rites and prayer, untold hermits to serve.
Like tendrils of smoke blew dawn and dusk—weightless, swift as grace.
Then night. Night was the triffid that prowled the mind's streets,
sucking every sense. Night when Gautama would exile
my will, his mouth sowing into my skin cobalt letters,
twenty-eight chapters, a thousand texts on women's dharma,
four varna, the rank and file of sins, the price of guile . . .
'Until late have I stayed awake, let me sleep awhile,'

even those sutra would plead, whilst I—frontispiece
for his wisdom, his virtue, his spells—craved release
from safety. From the words thrust in my veins, cauled in lore, rose
Shatananda, my husband's son. Another sainted one,

warm and tender as rime. But no more threnodies,
for you seek else: the reason for my eternal smear.
You may know the who, the what, the where-and-when: Indra, lord
of heaven, came in Gautama's guise, clamouring congress.
I'd laughed, undeceived: 'Such knaves, you gods that men revere!
A trace of the night remains; wait, let morning appear,

Ô heedless king, breach not occult walls from inside.
The sage and son walk in with dawn: through her chinks, slide
out unseen, unharmed.' Was it chagrin, fear or shades softer,
less certain, that made the rake blurt, 'I covet, never court;
win, with arms or wile. But this time, you shall decide.'
Truth and choice: two strangers, my whys. Greed stilled
at the edge of doom, the monarch bowed. And I claimed: the nape
of his neck, an instep, both palms, then the flanks, that groundswell
of lust . . . marked all with lips which had distilled
those half-grown dreams that could not be fulfilled.

I chose, yes, chose that once to become beloved.
I reclaimed this self. Of the rest, so much—smudged—spread
into legend: the spouse's fury, the son's desertion,
Indra's odium, my stigma as stone, then *redemption*.
Most, I let be. But rivers die from truths unsaid,
hence one more: Lord Rama did not restore
my form. I live as agate, granite, quartz—this, the blessing
I asked, and obtained: let me be igneous, everywhere.
Let me retrieve the lustrous dreams of yore.
Let me sow, in my sleep, those dreams once more.

**Bibliography**

—*Pachkanya: women of substance* by Pradip Bhattacharya
—*The Ramayana* by Valmiki (General Books LLC, 2010)
—*In Search of Sita: Revisiting Mythology* edited by Namita Gokhale & Malashri Lal (Yatra/Penguin Books, 2009).

# Katabasis

## *Liz Bourke*

*In quantum mechanics, uncertainty relations for time and energy are not constant.*

Forget me. Forget the body, rich
with sweat, pumping dark blood,
fighting its every breath—
the desperation of being born
and being born again
every hour pledged defiance
in the teeth, in the face,
of death's final silence.
*Noether's theorem states with respect*
*to continuous symmetry . . .*
*corresponding values are conserved in time.*

The moment of surrender, with or without grace.

When you're young you think death is
something that only happens to other people.

Fragments. A diaphragm, straining. Rasp and rise
the noise of everything you ever knew falling away
falling into vacuum.
*Bodies in motion remain in motion unless*
*some other force supervenes.*

Acid, it eats you away, cell by cell
memory by memory, sense by sense.
*Respiration is a katabolic reaction.*

*Katabasis:*

1. a going down

2. a great retreat

3. descent to the underworld

*After autolysis and putrefaction, the jaw lies unhinged and gaping. The sky, blue through the sockets of the skull, empty eyes. Every bone laid bare, every skeletal imperfection, every offence that left its mark in calcium and marrow.*

In the funeral parlour, the air stinks of dying flowers.
Decay papered over. Restless waiting hours.
These remaining hours.

Anticipate—I can't—the service
speaking with a dead tongue gone numb
gone breathless
mourners like carrion crows cawing
clawing clay out of your mouth
clawing earth out of your lungs.

# The Art of Flying

## *Georgina Bruce*

Maggie flies in the night. It's like swimming a breaststroke through the air. She can see for miles around, see her truck parked in the bay and the motorway winding in a charcoal line to the horizon. She loves the sweet purple heather, the peach-red sunrise. Currents of air buoy her, lift her, wave upon wave. When the sky lets go of her she falls like a feather, and lands in the dew-wet grass.

She's barefoot, dressed in jeans and a jumper. There is nothing to be scared of, she tells herself. This is the sort of thing that might happen in a dream. So she climbs the hill, digging her toes into the grass and soil. On the other side of the hill she sees her truck, and beyond that the mountains with their jagged tops of snow. Yesterday there had been eagles riding the air near the mountain peaks. Maggie had stopped on the hard shoulder to watch their elegant turns. She had the stereo on at full volume, playing canticles written by Hildegard von Bingen nearly a thousand years before.

*I, the fiery life of divine wisdom, I ignite the beauty of the plains, I sparkle the waters, I burn in the sun, and the moon, and the stars.*

The bleak morning pulls the day open and pale light falls across the hills. Maggie wishes the dream would pick her up and move her swiftly to her destination. Her body is stiff, and gets stiffer with every step.

At last she reaches the truck, but it is locked up and heavy blackout curtains drawn all around the cab windows. Only now does she start to feel panicky constrictions in her heart and stomach. She tells herself *wake up.* Slaps herself round the face with stinging hands.

She has the keys in her hand, but her fingers are too cold and clumsy to open the cab door. She is afraid she might find herself lying there in the back, asleep. Dreaming. Or dead. After some minutes of worrying at the lock, the door springs open. When she climbs into the cab, it is empty, of course.

* * *

She doesn't sleep the next night. The cargo has to get to Rakovski, a long haul down the Trakia Highway. She picks up her load of pallettes, making sure to check the contents carefully against the paperwork. The supervisor leans back against the cab, slowly smoking a cigarette and watching her through narrowed eyes.

When she can't drive any more, she parks in a bay and straps herself into the driver's seat. She slides the photograph of her daughter from under the mirror, and presses it to her heart, then props it up on the dashboard, next to the figurine of a man with the head of a dog. That is Saint Christopher, the patron saint of truckers.

She works on the problem of her night flight in little parcels of lucidity. Maybe she sleep walked, hit her head, was concussed, amnesiac. An epileptic seizure. Perhaps her cancer has come back, has spread to her brain. A myriad explanations present themselves for judgment, but none of them convince her. Perhaps it is a gift from God.

Perhaps it is a miracle.

The Church of the Highway holds a service under a large blue tarpaulin, rigged from the top of the bridge down to the grass verge at the side of the road. Under the tarpaulin are hundreds of wax candles, burning gold. The candle flames flicker and blur into teary shapes falling down the insides of Maggie's eyelids when she closes her eyes.

"Maggie," a voice says softly, into her ear.

Maggie jumps and turns towards the voice, fear spiking her blood. But it is only Gabriel, the church pastor.

"Are you okay?" He puts a hand on her shoulder. "I heard what happened."

"I'm okay," Maggie says. How else can she answer? No one speaks of her husband directly. As if to merely speak of him will cause the bruises to bloom on her skin, will cause her bones to break.

Gabriel leads her to a seat at the front of the church. He has to get ready for the service. Maggie sits on her hands, and shivers, perhaps with cold. She wishes her seat were a bit more comfortable, but knows that she would probably fall asleep if it was. There is a feeling of pressure in the back of her head, and her skull makes popping, creaking sounds, like it's contracting in the cold.

About twenty people are gathered under the tarpaulin. In the blue and gold space, with the rumble of traffic overhead, and the cold breaths of wind that sometimes blow around them, the church-goers become quiet and still. When Gabriel reappears, dressed in a white robe with an orange sunburst sash across his breast, he is transformed by ritual into something other than a man. He's the keeper of the mysteries. Light falls from his hands.

Maggie cannot catch her breath. Gabriel speaks, welcoming everybody, and his voice seems to swell and fill all of the space. It bursts from his chest, a wound of blinding light. It rises to the roof and breaks out like it's prickled with stars, exploding over the heads of the congregation. The voice rains fire on Maggie. She puts her hands over her head in frantic prayer, and the voice speaks to her and says, *I burn in the sun, and the moon, and the stars.*

She feels herself rising out of her chair. First her hair rises up, then her arms, pointing up to the tarpaulin roof. A hot snake of power muscles its way through her body. It pushes her up out of her chair, up above the congregation who are breathing heavy into the night. The voice is the breath. The voice is the fire. Maggie looks down and sees herself amongst the churchgoers, her body rigidly leaning forward. She is awash with tender pity for herself and in that moment of feeling, she is pulled back and lands inside herself with a jolt. She falls from her chair onto the ground.

"YOU NEED SLEEP," says Gabriel. "That's all. Nothing's wrong with you."

Maggie sips cold water from a plastic cup. It's too dark to see very clearly. They're sitting in Gabriel's cab. The Church is packed up in the back, and everyone else has gone home or driven on to their resting place or their next destination.

"I'm so tired. I'm losing my mind."

"No," says Gabriel. "Don't think that way. It's the breakup. It's stress. You work hard, you miss your daughter. You have a bad dream, and maybe you can't sleep well anymore, it's normal."

"I have to stop driving."

"Yes, of course. If you aren't sleeping."

"But is it from God? Is it a test? Does He want something from me?"

"I don't know, Maggie. But God gives comfort. Don't be afraid of sleeping. I will pray for you."

* * *

Maggie's body is a ruined country where everything lovely has been bombed out. Her chest is marked with a ragged white burn scar that pulls the flesh tight in ridges and craters. Her thighs are skinny, hollow at the top, and her hip bones jut out like shark fins. There is nowhere to touch Maggie's body that does not have some painful history. The doctor draws in a breath when she lifts Maggie's shirt up to press her stomach.

"It's come back, hasn't it?" Maggie tenses, and her stomach goes rigid.

"Breathe!" The doctor tells her, pushing on her belly. "There's nothing wrong with you. You're fine. Just a bit thin."

Dr. Lesley is the company doctor; an elegant woman with short, manicured nails and grey hair cut like a man's. It was Dr. Lesley who helped Maggie gather the strength to leave her husband. It was she who took her to the hospital after he found her again and beat her bloody.

"I've brought you something," says Maggie, after the examination, when they are sitting either side of Dr. Lesley's desk. She reaches into the pocket of her leather jacket and pulls out a little wooden figurine: a man with the head of a dog.

Dr. Lesley takes the figurine and smiles. Saint Christopher, the patron saint of truckers, is also the patron saint of those who suffer from toothache. Maggie and Dr. Lesley know all the saints, on account of them both having had a Catholic schooling, and Saint Christopher is their favourite.

"Please don't worry," says Dr. Lesley. "Just take care of yourself."

She signs the certificate that says Maggie is fit to work.

There is a convent at Ebstorf, and the nuns there watch over a map. It's a map of two worlds: a portrait of their faith, and a geographical picture. The original map burned in 1943, says the sign, but the nuns made a very detailed and faithful copy. Maggie is allowed to stand for an hour in front of it. The colours swim before her, red and blue and black, and the images seem to move. Creatures rear up on their hind legs, villages crumble to dust, rivers flow in wavy blue lines; and Christ encompasses everything in an infinite embrace. His steely gaze falls on Maggie and ignites her skin. The white scar on her chest flames and burns.

*I am so afraid.* She prays for something, she's not sure what. Some comfort.

Her cargo is bound for Munich, and she cannot stay for much longer. It is cold and snow is forecast. As she stands to leave, one of the nuns enters the room. She is old, Maggie sees. Her face is a map of lines.

"We are closing the viewing, I'm sorry," she says. Her voice is soft and tremulous.

"I'm sorry," says Maggie. "It's so beautiful."

"Yes." The nun smiles. "It is so very interesting, I think. Are you a Catholic?"

Maggie nods, and the nun smiles again. When they walk out of the room, the nun guides her, holding gently on to her elbow, as if Maggie is the elderly one.

"It is a wonderful thing," says the nun.

Maggie says, "I'm dying, you see." Why did she say that? She is embarrassed and wishes she hadn't blurted it out, but the nun appears to consider her statement carefully.

"Death is just one more thing we must do," she says. "I will pray for you."

Maggie walks back to her cab, her hips aching from the cold. What a thing it is to be so old at forty-two, she thinks. And she wonders if dying is like flying in the night.

HER DAUGHTER CALLS while Maggie is eating her sandwiches in a lay-by near Bad Bevensen. It has already started to snow. She has the heaters on full blast, and is wearing her jacket that feels like being wrapped up in a sleeping bag.

"He's out," says Cara. "Out on bail. Fuck's sake."

Maggie flinches at Cara's bad language, or is it at the bad news? She's not sure.

"Mum, I think you should come home."

"Maybe." It's not safe anywhere now. Not back in England, not with Cara, not on the road. But he doesn't know the rigs like she does. He was only ever a small-timer in the business, never even drove an eighteen-wheeler. He won't get very far if he comes looking for her. Truckers look after their own.

"If he comes here, I'm going to kill him," says Cara.

"Cara. Don't say that. He's probably not even allowed to be in the same city."

"I fucking mean it. I'm serious. And if he lays a hand on you." She doesn't finish her sentence.

"Don't swear, love. He's not going to get anywhere near me, or you, so stop worrying. I don't want you to worry."

"Please come home, Mum," Cara says. She sounds so heart-breakingly young that Maggie has to fight back tears.

"I will, darling, I will come home soon. I'll be home before you know it."

After the phone call, Maggie starts up the engine. The snow is coming thick and fast now. She drives carefully, unable to see far ahead, feeling like a giant in the massive rig, high above the rest of the traffic.

SHE DREAMS THAT Saint Christopher is running beside her, his tongue hanging from his jaws, his long nose pushed up in the air.

*Good boy, good . . .*

A struggle to get her breath, and she yanks herself upright. Where am I? The cocooning whiteness of snow . . . But she is warm, dry. She changes focus: she is in the cab, she's safe.

The windscreen is shrouded in snow, obscuring any view. She rolls down the window. Four other rigs are pulled up nearby, but she doesn't recognise any of them. She leans out to knock snow off her windscreen. From across the lay-by, she hears music.

Gabriel's little truck is almost hidden behind a massive artic. It looks like a sliver of Christmas, lit up in gold and blue, red and silver. Maggie puts coffee, chocolates, and cigarettes into her pockets, and trudges through the deep snow.

"I can't believe it," she says, hugging Gabriel. "I heard the music and I knew it must be you."

"Been here all night. I don't like to drive in bad weather. You too, it's dangerous driving in the snow."

"Maybe. I'll give it a couple of hours, anyway. We can visit."

They sit in the truck. Maggie tries to eat the chocolates, nibbling away at the edges, but they don't taste of anything.

Gabriel leans in so she can hear him over the whirr of the heater. "I'm worried for you. I heard he's out of prison."

"You heard already? Has he been looking for me?"

"Don't think so. He has some friends on the road still. A few. What are you thinking?"

Maggie is staring at her hands. They are shaking. After a minute she says, "I'm sick, Gabe. I shouldn't be driving. I can't drive anymore, I really can't. But I don't know what else to do."

Gabriel takes her hands in his. "The cancer?"

"The doctor said no, she said it's gone. She said I'm fine. But I can feel it inside me. I'm dying, Gabriel. I know I am."

"Oh, Maggie," he says. His hand tightens around hers.

They pray together all morning, until Maggie sees the colours rising from Gabriel, blue and gold, red and silver, and the fiery words burn over her. She lets him massage her hands, which are stiff and cold. Her fingers warm under his gentle ministrations, and she feels them grow soft and strong, young again.

"There are so many miracles," she whispers, and the Pastor cries and kisses her fingers.

THEY HEAR ABOUT him in Gdansk; a trucker there radios Maggie to let her know. He's driving a baby rig around for one of his old friends; he never could handle an artic. *Let him come,* thinks Maggie. *Let him come and it will all be over.*

She turns in her last cargo in Varna and drives back to Germany. She wants to get to Ebstorf if she can, to see the map again and drink in its strange beauty. It's cold everywhere, but she hardly feels it now. She has stopped sleeping, stopped eating, no longer defecates, even. Sometimes, when she's driving, she loses her body, and her consciousness drifts into the engine of the rig. Her wheels turn, and her gears change up and down, smooth and flowing like breathing in and out.

At a rest stop near Munich, she telephones Cara and tells her she's coming home to England. She'll be back very soon, she says.

"Has he found you?" Cara asks. "Does he know where you are?"

"I won't let him get anywhere near me."

"I'm scared for you," says Cara.

"I love you," says Maggie. "You're my wonderful daughter. I'm so proud of you. And I'm so sorry for everything."

"Don't be daft, Mum," says Cara. "I can't wait for you to come back."

Maggie winds down her window, and throws her cab keys out into the ditch. No more of that. No more. Saint Christopher barks once from the back of the cab, and she smiles, and draws the blackout curtains all around. She climbs over onto the thin mattress, and curls up next to him. His soft ears flicker against her face. She clutches her wooden rosary and her photograph of her daughter, which she kisses before she closes her eyes.

The air is so cold that when she flies through the clear night, it shatters and falls to the ground in a tinkling rush. Below her, the whole world is spread out in vivid red and blue and black. The world is made of soft vellum, sewn together, embroidered with bold threads. Creatures rear up and canter through the landscapes: a monster with the head of a snake and the body of a lorry charges towards a village made of wheels. A gold and blue church rises luminous on a white plain. The moon burns with white fire and bursts with beams of light, and the voice of the world takes her breath, *I, I, yes, I, the fiery life of divine wisdom, I ignite the beauty of the plains, I sparkle the waters, I burn in the sun, and the moon, and the stars.*

A dog barks, rhythmically yapping into the night. Maggie soars into the sparkling darkness, flying home at last.

# Dreams of Bone

*Christina Sng*

I am bone tired and weary.
These calcified white twigs
Thud dully as they collide,

Collapsing
Into an inverted pyramid,
Remnant of an hourglass

Clasped in a small hand,
Tiny as a bird's, eyes
Saucer-wide, blinking.

I stay by the quiet
Oasis in the sands,
The silent waterfall

With clear blue water
I can breathe in.
I devour serenity

In that old cabin
Sitting on the lip of the lake,
Ebbing over crystalline water

As green grass
Unrolls like a lazy carpet
Over the sighing sand.

Trees emerge, triumphant
From the damp
Dew-drenched grass,

Branches outstretched,
Embracing the sun—
Their long lost friend.

I catch the light
On my pale death skin,
Torched from summer's kiss,

While swirling black holes
Grind craters into my flesh,
Like exhausted match tips

After a brief, fierce burn.
These scorched blooms,
Autumn's red roses

Once plump and succulent;
Green fields of abundance,
Now oases in winter:

The outcasts of the desert;
The ice sculpture in the fire.
And in the sunshine,

I shatter,
Scattering ash and ice
Over the water;

The cradle of life:
The place of new beginnings.
The land of a dreamless sleep.

# India Pale Angel

## *Robert Davies*

Elizabeth Court's angel died over the weekend, but it wasn't until Wednesday that she could smell its sweet, luminous decay. She had assumed her Monday morning hangover was just taking time to uncoil itself from inside her skull, but soon realized that instead of the aching brain that filled the early coffee-drip hours of the workweek it was her angel's corpse weighing her down. Dragged behind her, it got stuck in elevator doors and subway turnstiles and made dogs tug at their leashes and piss in uncertain fear. Escalator teeth bit harshly at the feathers until the wings resembled plucked chicken skin. The angel's samite robes dragged on the floor, mud stained and torn.

WITH A NAME like Inexplicable Cain, it seems his dark proclivities were set in stone as soon as the ink dried on the birth certificate, and thus perhaps you can find some small measure of forgiveness for him. I can, for surely his given name guided his wet, glinting hands through many warm lengths of innards and cooling wombs. He spent his speechless years inside a Skinner Box. When his legs grew so much that his pale knees worried into his eye sockets as he crouched, he was moved into a Skinner Room. He then was given free reign of a locked House Without Windows and given wondrous, shivering playmates with whom to play. The toys of his childhood were stainless steel blades, scalpels, and specula that reeked of rubbing alcohol and the anxious sweat of his tongueless nannies.

Then he found the key.

STEPHEN BRADDOCK, STILL drunk, murmurs in the darkness, fitfully sleeping over a thousand million words at Shakespeare and Company in Paris.

* * *

The used bookstore on the corner is never there when you want it to be. Every time you look for a bookstore in Harvard Square, you forget quite where it is, although it always involves at least ten steps up some stone steps and a turn or two down a narrow alleyway, and then at least thirteen steps down. It is always underground, except when it is not, and the sun that streams through the windows into the tiger cat's face is one we have seen before.

The books lining the shelves are always in disarray; Clarissa, whose job it is to keep them straight, paints her ragged fingernails black, tells stupid little lies, and sticks needles in between her toes. She is kneeling over there, trying to decide if R coming after Q is really the best way to do things, and wondering if her self-published book of poetry *Kama Sutra for Quadriplegics* will ever sell. Clarissa ignores Elizabeth, indeed studiously ignores anyone not reeking of patchouli or inked with at least one mythical beast. She does not even see the decaying angel draped across the table piled with oversized cookbooks, knocking Rachael Ray and Anthony Bourdain to the ground.

An astronomy book with a crater-pocked Moon on its dust cover looks slightly out of place. It is up there beside a coffee table book on Parisian architecture, the moonlit stones of Notre Dame shrouded in clouds on its face. Elizabeth tries to ignore the book and its misplaced Moon, but, of course, she can't. She reaches up for it. It is awkward at first, as the angel weighs her down and makes her lower back ache, but she stretches and manages to grab the book with the tips of her fingers. It is insanely heavy, its weight almost tidal. She shifts it down one shelf and slightly to the right, where it seems to belong. For a brief moment, Elizabeth smells the silver of midnight Parisian rain and hears the brass wails of distant jazz.

She finds a paperback collection of Gene Wolfe stories and slips it into her coat pocket. A few bent angel feathers fall from her coat, but only Marcel Marceau notices, and as a cat he really doesn't care. His sleep has been disturbed enough today, thank you. He wants her, her stolen book, and her dead angel gone. Now. His eyes close with feline disdain.

Elizabeth crosses the street against the light, and her angel is nearly run over by a taxi. She ignores the horn. She walks onto the grass, looking for a comfortable place to read.

When Elizabeth sits on the lawn, she knows she has to be careful; an angel's corpse is something that acorns and green grass dream of often. In rot, an angel's flesh is as rich and fecund as any soil known. Although it should be said that few soils have ever burnt their palms on the hilt of flaming swords or cast down impregnable desert-baked walls with a mere whisper or a trumpet blast, but it is true in as much as it is.

Inexplicable Cain scans the crowd, knowing that the time has come again. He has trimmed his nails to the quick and shaved himself from head to toe. He clasps his pale hands and cracks his knuckles. And like that moment a key snaps perfectly into a lock, he sees Elizabeth sitting on the ground, and everything in this world of ours ceases to exist.

The summer air is languorous and a bright-eyed girl is strumming an acoustic guitar and singing Joni Mitchell songs. Because the stories are byzantine and beautiful, and because her heart is broken, Elizabeth sits on the grass a moment too long. She is remembering old boyfriends, trying to forget one in particular, and, their patience ended, the grass and the tree roots quickly overcome her angel, spreading greedily, exploding in green, cellulosic joy.

An immense brown elm bursts from the angel's chest and spirals upward, unfurling branches feathered with whispering green leaves that blot out the afternoon sun.

Elizabeth tries to stand, but can't move. Inexplicable Cain tries to run, but can't move. Stephen tries to awaken, but can't move.

The bright-eyed girl begins another Joni Mitchell song.

A tall man in a well-tailored business suit stops before the singing girl and takes a coin from her worn guitar case. He spiders across the lawn and gives it to Elizabeth. Not a nickel or a quarter, but a coin all the same. He hesitates for a moment, as though waiting for his fortune to be told. This Elizabeth cannot do, much to her regret, wishing she could do something in return for his kindness. She frowns. She could tell him his past, though, for she can do that rather well. But for a long moment, held down as she is by the angel, her memories, and the vigorous, leafy tree, she has forgotten how to speak, has forgotten the mad intricacies of the alphabet and the glottal stop, and, dispirited, the tall man walks away.

Inexplicable Cain, leaning against a tree, is tempted to follow the tall man and show him the secret joys of flensing. But Inexplicable knows that way leads to madness. The girl is the only one who will set him free. He turns to watch her move, praying she will not turn around and walk the other way.

It is so easy to get lost in the heart of the big city, Elizabeth knows, but it is easier still to get lost sitting on sun-warmed grass with a stolen book of stories. She watches strangers pass by, counting those that have cancer and don't even know it. She gives people newer, better names. She covets quirky shoes, and she waits for the first drops of the inevitable rain.

When the rain comes, there are many places in Harvard Square to run to, mostly underground, except when they are not. Elizabeth remembers that John Harvard's Brew House has Willey's IPA on tap this week. It is rather delicious with an order of fried zucchini sticks. Slumbrew Flagraiser is likely on tap at Grendel's, and, in summer, there is always Harpoon IPA at Legal's.

A pale man in a perfect black suit is leaning against a tree, watching her. Elizabeth blinks and he is no longer there. Where he had stood there is just the barest suggestion of presence, the silhouette of appetite. She blinks again and doubts herself.

Elizabeth then remembers the tall man's past. His wife Moira, horse-faced and kind, died in childbirth; he is broken inside, but still manages to name the baby Stephen, after her father's father, and the boy spends a mute childhood reading Marvel comic books and murdering butterflies by the thousands. He slips through the cracks at high school and three years of college before falling in love and then fleeing. He finds himself shivering in a musty sleeping bag on the third floor of Shakespeare and Company on the bank of the Seine, his ragged fingernails stained burgundy with wine and ink, his Moleskines stuffed with crude ink sketches of those moments when people decide to turn around and walk the other way.

It is just past midnight, and Stephen, in the mood for perhaps another Brasserie du Mont Salève IPA, stands up and makes his way through the snoring, dreaming, wine-blessed, trembling shapes that keep the floor from floating heavenward. He sneaks down the stairs, slips a Moorcock from the shelves, stamps it quietly, leaves a five-euro note on the counter. The door opens into the cold glistening rainy Parisian night.

He walks the few steps to the Petit Pont and crosses over to the Île de la Cité along the Rue de Notre Dame, wet gargoyles shivering in the vast heights, their throats phlegmed with fog and mist. He fumbles in his jacket for his favorite pen, his only pen. He remembers too late that he lent it to a Czech girl at La Caveau de la Huchette so she could write down a fake phone number for some clueless guy with a technicolor bestiary tattooed on each forearm. It is a jazzy set of numbers slightly out of sync with her real number, adding one to the first digit, subtracting one from the next, and so on, throwing in a zero on a whim because the worn, black saxophonist is sucking in air and blowing out very early Trane, and the third bottle of wine is getting warm, and the air is too, too much, and your friend left with that guy with the just right jeans, and you need to hear one more song, one more song, one more song. She had said she would give it right back, but, well, we all know the type.

The moon shifts ever so slightly, as though moved, and the perfect dust of old books fills the air and a cat meows, and the rain and winds die down. It is no longer night. The unexpected sun is warm. Stephen wonders if he has already awoken, but when he see the Charles River in Cambridge, Massachusetts, running beneath him he is sure that he has never really been asleep.

He runs across Memorial Drive, and heads up JFK Street, hoping beyond hope that he can remember English.

Pulled from her nap, Clarissa reaches for the ringing phone.

The guy on the other end is drunk and speaking in French about caves, dancing, and tattoos.

It is a wrong number, but she no longer cares.

Elizabeth watches Stephen as he walks by. His is the kind of beauty that breaks bones she thinks, as she did the first time she saw him, and then she changes her mind. Everything around him seems to shimmer, as though his breath were the gauzy heat of mirage, as though the brick sidewalk and the crowded coffee shop, the cluttered magazine stall, and the hipster clothes boutique before him melt, warp, and are sucked through his wrists only to then spill from the wounds at his ankles, swelling and popping back to solidity behind him just as they had been before he ever walked by, with the windows perhaps a bit more shiny, the bricks a shade darker. She turns away from him as though from the noonday sun.

It then occurs to her that there is no reason why she cannot carry an angel, even a dead angel, and the forest that now flourishes from its chest, and all the trees, and the gray birds and the red-chested ones and the baby blue eggs that crowd the nests. No reason at all, so she stands up. She begins to wonder whether not eating for a few days was the best course of action, and, feeling ravenous, decides to go underground to Grendel's Den to get some fiery shrimp sambal and a CBC Spring Training IPA.

Inexplicable Cain watches her move, and it is a moment he savors. The urgency of her movements speaks to him, and he gnaws his tongue because he really needs to taste some blood. He considers following her underground, but thinks better of it. He slips himself into an empty doorway and moves the razor blades from his right pocket to the left. He will wait until nightfall, and then they will meet.

She worries her way down the narrow stairway, but has trouble fitting through the door, what with her dead angel, the oaks, the flock, the nests, the eggs and all. She perseveres and manages at last, turning this way and then that to get the wooden green adumbration of branches through the door. There is an empty stool at the bar, praise highly the god of hops, and, for ten minutes longer, the food is half-price. She orders her IPA and sips it gingerly. There is a sharp chip at the rim. A sign over the bar reads "No Bud. No Coors. No Coors Lite. No Bud Lite. No Miller. No Michelob. BASTA" She does not know what "BASTA" means.

A waitress with pendulous breasts trips over one of the tree's wandering roots, nearly dropping her glass-laden tray, and Elizabeth turns to apologize but the words are stopped in her throat. Stephen is sitting by himself across the bar and he is looking at her, and his tree is far bigger than hers, its branches crashing through the ceiling. His decaying angel is almost gone. The wineglass in his stained fingers is a dwindling sunlit ruby. He looks away too quickly, but can't hide his embarrassed grin.

Somehow he looks younger than he did. No, his eyes look older.

There is in every movement the suggestion of something held back, of some alternative breath or word that would change everything. As in the womb there is the promise of a child, and in the seed the promise of the rose, so is there in every word the promise of new language, and perhaps even new understanding. Elizabeth wants to say something to him, anything, but everything she thinks of has been said before.

The birds from her tree and perhaps a few from his have lined themselves up on the low windowsills on either side of the fireplace, watching the feet of passersby. One dove fixates on a nacho chip on the floor.

She decides to say nothing. It is just easier this way, easier to walk away. She throws back the last sip of IPA, slicing her lip and tasting blood, stands, leaves a twenty on the counter, and turns to the door. Her angel almost refuses to budge, but Elizabeth is determined. She moves as though she were pulling the entirety of creation behind her. The night air is getting cold and it looks like rain.

Inexplicable Cain is watching her from the shadows, his heart pounding with a ferocity that astounds him.

Stephen, frozen, watches her go. He then knows this will end. There isn't much time. He opens his Moleskine, smoothes the last empty page, and reaches into his pocket. He loudly curses drunk Czech girls. He stands to call out to Elizabeth, to say something witty or unusual, something that will make her stay, but he knocks his bag to the floor, spilling everything, his Moleskine splaying open, torn ticket stubs, bent paper clips, foreign coins, expired condoms, out-of-date train schedules, and postage stamps scattering.

A long, limp feather juts from his angel's broken wing. Stephen quickly plucks it and spears his palm with the quill, worrying it around until the blood is plentiful. He finds that special page, that empty, dog-eared page, and begins to furiously draw, hoping there is enough time for one last sketch.

# a recipe

*Lynette Mejía*

Start with herb.
They expect time
as they are used to
withering.
Crush, chew, extract
the juices until they bleed,
blend into intention. You
may need to use teeth.

Mix in mineral.
Break along planes,
cleave and fracture,
pulverize,
destroy in the service of creation.
Add fire if you must.

This is where the skill
severs art
from artifice;
where thought blooms a dread
flower becoming deed.

Stir carefully.
Simmer in the blood
of an enemy. Drink,
absorb, ascribe
meaning to the sacrifice.
Timing is everything.

# Anna They Have Killed

## *Jennifer Crow*

Life spools across the tiles, red words they whispered
As they pulled the trigger. Loose tongues must be punished
And silence must come to the brave. However many battles
She witnessed, however many dead names she inscribed
On the walls of the world, she could not guard her own heart
From the fateful brass and powder. Death jangles
In the empty lobby where burned-out bulbs leave shadows
Between doors. Death rides in long black cars and slides
Across the pavement on fine leather and shoots its cuffs
Before the fatal, fateful blast. We know its face well enough,
Though not one soul will bear witness.

She carried the poison in her blood, the tales told
Of murder, of torture, of sparking wires thrust into the heart
Of a nation. She carried poison from a cup of tea,
A cup of hate pressed into her hand by the secret enemy.
Every face hides an enemy, a hunger without peace.
You can eat in this brave new world of open markets,
Eat and never be filled, never quiet the rumbling
That wells up out of the tundra, the forest, the vast cold sea.
You can give all your coins, all those crumpled paper bills,
And still crave a closed loop, a surcease, a cease-fire.

Someone will bury the story, slit its throat, fire
A bullet of lies into its heart and let it fall, silenced.
Everyone knows already, though they never look
At the ink stains, the poisoned dreams. They know already
The pointed finger will be sliced off.
A tsar still rules old Moskva, and his men
Ride with broom and dog's head, ride
Out of the night and burn the truth in the fields.

Her fingers curl a little against the cool tiles, stretch
As if to grasp truth one last time. She caught the hem
Of the gods, the fearful robe that covers
The terrible deeds of men, and tried to pull it aside.
But the gods that dwell between the Dnieper and the Volga,
The old powers of fear and waste, will not turn aside
For the fearless. They lay claim on blood and fire
And draw a cloak over her dimming eyes.

# The Two Annies of Windale Road

## *Patty Templeton*

Two elderly women stood twenty paces apart on the crowded, shrub-edged lawn of the Windale Care and Rehabilitation Center. Two women with tight lips and pistols on creaking hips.

Shirley Connet was the owner of seventy-six years and Marlene Fenn had seventy-nine. Both possessed the medically noted, grandiose delusion that they were Annie Oakley.

Late October leaves scattered past wheelchairs. Reverent onlookers rubbed palms together at patio tables. Aimless walkabouts and patients of assorted debilitating afflictions knew better than to congregate to the north or south, given the possibility of stray bullets.

Marlene's thin, red hair uncurled with the breeze.

Shirley's left eye squinted.

A line of three dragonflies flew between the women and settled on fallen seeds at the base of a leaning sunflower.

The staff of Windale Care and Rehab devoured several boxes of Girl Scout cookies strategically placed in the break room far from the commons' window.

That there were two Little Miss Sure Shots did not distress either woman. Yes, this was a shootout. A showdown. A quick draw. But the bloody intent was not over the Oakley name.

It was the gaps.

Before Marlene and Shirley ever spoke about the gaps, they met because of "The Cottage Cheese Incident."

Shirley ate oatmeal at an empty table in the Windale breakfast hall.

Marlene grazed the buffet in tall-heeled cowboy boots. They did Marlene's corns no good and her back ached, but Marlene would quit wearing make-up before she quit wearing her fake-alligator boots, and Marlene wasn't going to quit lipstick this side of the six foot drop. Besides, boots made her taller, easier for an audience to appreciate.

Shirley noticed Marlene. How could you not notice her? All that blue fringe and matching eye shadow. Shirley was not jealous of the flash, but she did miss the days when arthritis had not made button-down shirts a bother. Shirley tipped her Stetson over her forehead and kept her eyes on the tabletop.

Shirley was eating sweet cantaloupe meat when the yelling started.

"What's in this?" Marlene Fenn howled at a nurse.

"Meds. Eat it," the nurse said. He was skinny. He hadn't shaved. All he wanted was to get through the shift without a shit stain somewhere on his scrubs. These old people shit themselves all the time and got it on their hands and then it was as mandatory as dogs licking assholes that the fossils shared their shit with you.

"No," Marlene said.

"It'll calm you down."

The nurse rubbed his scruff.

Murmurs began in the breakfast hall. *Eat it. Go on. Don't do it. Quit your bitchin'.*

Marlene Fenn did not need medication. She needed her gun.

Shirley's forehead tensed and her fists clenched as she watched the pair.

The nurse nodded at two orderlies leaning by the buffet counter.

Marlene Fenn dumped her cottage cheese over the nurse's head.

The nurse grabbed Marlene's hand and shoulders.

"Get your paws off me," Marlene said and kicked the nurse in the shin.

The two orderlies ran.

The nurse didn't know what to do and the cottage cheese plopped through his eyelashes.

Shirley Connet stood up. She wasn't afraid of righting a wrong. Ain't no man should put his hands on a lady.

All heck broke loose.

How two old women could carry on like that and not die could only be explained by witchery (so said the Baptist Art Club). Marlene busted a heel. Shirley's Velcro shoes were stained in blueberry yogurt and so was her Stetson. The nurse broke his pinky from an undecipherable hit. Marlene had a fistful of an orderly's hair that would never grow back. Bruised necks. Cracked dentures. The ceiling tiles were permanently stained in ranchero sauce. All through the ruckus, the women smiled. Never let the audience know when something has gone wide of the mark, that's what Buffalo Bill had said.

Windale Care and Rehab had a zero tolerance policy for violent outbursts. The Connet and Fenn families begged second chances. The gaps were mentioned. Delusions were fine, but neither family had the sufferance for early onset Alzheimer's. The endurance. The tolerance for what it would become. The time off of work. They appealed to Windale's board while Shirley and Marlene sat with crossed arms. Treatment was implored rather than expulsion. An exploratory committee examined the issue. Donations were given. A new Windale Therapeutic wing was designed.

It was in mandatory therapy sessions that Shirley Connet and Marlene Fenn became closer than a cuff and a button.

DOCTOR CHUCK LED all Elder Care Emotions First group therapy sessions at Windale Care and Rehab. Doctor Chuck had a wrinkled forehead that questioned and underestimated you as you spoke. He polished his shoes each morning. He wore a tie and sweater-vest every day. His desk was stacked with Oliver Sacks's books. Doctor Chuck would place *The Man Who Mistook his Wife for a Hat* in the center of his flat desk calendar. He'd then put his forehead on the cover for prolonged periods. It made Doctor Chuck feel better. Important. Centered.

He was a man easily over-taxed by details, but obsessed with collecting them. He had files on both Shirley Connet and Marlene Fenn.

Doctor Chuck found that Ms. Shirley Connet often sat in her room and watched a crack in the windowpane spider outward. When asked if she liked being alone, Shirley responded, "I get angry around people." The word *apocalyptic* appeared in a previous Connet file. Shirley chaired up for meals with C4 spinal cord injury patients because, quote, "They don't talk." She avoided the television room except when informed of a *Dark Shadows* or *Top Chef* marathon. She won every gin rummy game she played. She was fond of Nurse Edward Yee, whom she referred to as Eddy. When asked why she liked Eddy, Shirley responded, "He's a queer, but he pencils my eyebrows in even-handed and if I was friends with Sitting Bull and his redmen, why for rope can't I be comrades with a nance? He's a good egg."

What wasn't noted in Doctor Chuck's file was that Shirley loved Eddy because he didn't snoop and because he didn't snoop he didn't know that Shirley had a gun in a shoebox hidden under her desk. Shirley found that she remembered things better when she held a gun in her hand.

Marlene had an equally detailed file. Someone had scribbled out *total bitch* in the side notes. In Doctor Chuck's observations, Ms. Fenn was not shy to recall her mother identifying her as everything from Jezebel to trash-walker. Quote, "I like a good romp in the closet as much as any gal and I don't care who can see that truth in the waggle in my walk. 'Sides what's the worth of a fringed outfit if you can't shake what's in it?" Doctor Chuck also noted that Ms. Fenn thought Windale had much too much beige paint and she, ". . . didn't like sitting with drooping old horndogs in the TV room when she could be out romancing the young and firm at the Dollar Mart." It was previously noted on Marlene's chart that she requested a day pass to go to the shooting range. When denied she berated the staff as "wingdings" that couldn't understand ". . . the obligations and the expectations of Wild Bill Cody."

Doctor Chuck's file on Marlene was missing the key fact that she traded a strong-armed patient named Benson, down in room 204, a tad of fringe shaking for a .22 mini-revolver.

Doctor Chuck wanted to write a profile of the two Annie Oakleys. He imagined awards. He pictured shaking Oliver Sacks's hand, which Doctor Chuck believed would be manicured. There'd be two shakes downward, a smile and business cards exchanged.

As expected, at their first Elder Care Emotions First session both Shirley Connet and Marlene Fenn were argumentative. Doctor Chuck's semicircle was converted into the therapeutic equivalent of an Annie Oakley PBS special.

"Shirley, why don't you start today's session by introducing yourself," Doctor Chuck said.

Heads around the semicircle twisted to Shirley.

"You know my name," Shirley said as she made knotted martyrs of her hands.

"Ahh, but tell the group."

"I was born Phoebe Ann Mosey on August 13, 1860," Shirley stated.

Doctor Chuck took notes.

Marlene stood.

"Are you saying you're Annie Oakley?" Marlene asked and paced around the room, lighting up a cigarette.

"Ms. Fenn, there is no smoking," Doctor Chuck said.

Marlene continued to smoke.

"Ms. Oakley, there is no smoking."

Marlene put her cigarette out in a potted plant and leaned on her chair. She wore a spangled green v-neck sweater. There was a bullet scar near her collarbone.

"You have a dog?" Marlene asked Shirley.

"Dave," Shirley answered.

"Perhaps we should discuss 'The Cottage Cheese Incident'," Doctor Chuck suggested.

This suggestion was ignored.

"Do you have a husband?" Marlene asked.

"I met Frank after I walloped him in a shooting contest," Shirley said.

Shirley asked Marlene, "You ever meet Buffalo Bill Cody?"

"Toured on the Wild West circuit 'bout seventeen years, didn't I?" Marlene said.

"I had a train wreck," Shirley said.

"Me too. 1901. Partial paralysis and five operations. But I'm still walkin', ain't I?" Marlene said.

"You're Annie Oakley?" Shirley asked.

"Seems like we both are," Marlene said.

It was here that Rudy, an Elder Care Emotions First session junky, jumped in. He tugged on his long socks underneath his rolled trousers.

"Doctor Chuck, my family hasn't come to see me in two weeks."

Doctor Chuck nodded.

Semicirclers nodded.

Marlene fought back a cruel laugh.

Shirley took the moment to close her eyes and process her new friend.

"Rudy, that's your name, right?" Marlene asked.

"Yep."

"Rudy, I'll bust you up. My gal and I were talking here."

Rudy looked at Doctor Chuck for help.

Doctor Chuck looked at Marlene for intentions.

Marlene lit up another cigarette.

The session spiraled downward from there. Doctor Chuck lost control. Marlene smoked a total of eleven cigarettes. Shirley rubbed a worry-hole into her sweater sleeve.

It took four months, but Marlene Fenn and Shirley Connet caused the white flag and resignation of Doctor Chuck. They never gave him written permission for his dueling Annie Oakleys profile.

Sessions were cancelled until a new therapist was hired.

"Don't need no Elder Care, shmelder care," Marlene said.

The ladies saved the real talking for their quiet times together.

Marlene stubbed out her cigarette on the patio table.

Shirley smoothed her slacks.

Someone slammed a horn in the parking lot.

"Do you forget things?" Marlene asked.

"Forget things how?" Shirley said.

"I can remember my first day at the Wild West and I can't remember if I had apple juice this morning. You ever forget things, girl?" Marlene asked.

"Sometimes I'm standing in front of the buzz-in guest door and I don't know how I got there," Shirley offered.

"How old are you?" Marlene asked.

"What now?" Shirley shyly looked at her nails.

"I'm eighty in December. Eighty. Now I don't know why I know that I'll be eighty in December and I can't remember if I ever had kids." Marlene blushed, but she kept her smile on.

"I can see the faces of people sitting in the front row when I dimmed the flame off a candle from a shot over my shoulder thirty years back and I don't remember how long ago I came here," Shirley admitted.

"I bet you could yet hit six holes in a playing card before it hit the ground," Marlene praised.

"And I believe you could still smite a dime tossed into a glare from over ninety feet," Shirley regarded.

"There are gaps." Marlene said.

"Little gaps," Shirley agreed.

"Every day there are more," Marlene said.

"Too many," Shirley said.

"I don't want to end this way," Marlene said.

"Which way?" Shirley asked.

"In a slow fizzle and outta my gourd."

Shirley closed eyes and thought on this.

"It doesn't have to end this way," Marlene said.

"Then how?" Shirley asked.

Marlene took Shirley's hand and they talked it over.

THE BACK LAWN of Windale Care and Rehab was more twigs, dirt and dead leaves than greenery. It had briefly rained. The ground was soft. The nearby highway hummed. Worms sorted around. The sky was a plate of grey clouds.

Shirley and Marlene stood twenty paces apart.

The congregation of onlookers knuckle cracked and foot shuffled.

Marlene's nails were a fresh coat of purple. They matched her eye shadow and her fringe. She wore her fake alligator boots. Shirley had mended the heel for her.

Shirley's nails held their usual French manicure and matched her cream cardigan perfectly. She wore beige flats that Marlene had painted in glitter in the art studio. Each woman had a letter in her pocket. A gun at her hip.

Over several months, Marlene and Shirley had measured the gaps.

The gaps had turned to clefts and would turn to chasms.

There was only worse and worser.

Neither woman wanted to miss themselves anymore.

Marlene and Shirley made a choice.

Calm hands on guns.

Someone threw a dime in the air.

The three dragonflies watched from under the sunflower.

Shirley and Marlene fired when the coin touched dirt.

Each woman hit the other in the heart.

Shirley died first. Marlene two breaths after.

Each was smiling.

The knitters went back inside. The alcoholics hid behind the shed. The pill-poppers went to their evening meetings. The staff quit eating cookies at the sound of gunfire.

The police couldn't believe that two old biddies had such good aim.

# Zora Neale Hurston Meets Felicia Felix-Mentor on the Road

*J.C. Runolfson*

She is being erased.
She can see it in those who swore
they knew her at first
her father, her husband, her neighbors.
We were mistaken, they say now
their eyes fixed past her.
It was a mistake.
Again she is taken from her home and
expected not to notice
but there is no draught to force forgetting.
They treat her as a horse
without a rider,
what is there to forget?

But she remembers
some things now,
remembered enough to come home
even if the very earth from which she was wrested
no longer wants her.
The strangers want her
the doctors and priests and storytellers
all of them unwilling to accept a mistake
unless it is theirs.
Here comes one now, on the road toward her
camera in hand.
She doesn't allow many pictures,
people use them as an excuse
not to look at her
not to see the truth of her there,
riding herself as best she can
when that was never meant to be the way.

They will do this to you too,
she wants to tell this storyteller,
whose picture she will allow because it will
be taken by dark woman's hands
and it will be on the road
and this one is certain it was no mistake,
knows a little something about riding
and being ridden.
They will erase you.
They will dismiss you,
a horse and no rider.
They will bury you.
She wants, but she hasn't the words anymore,
those were left far to the north,
on another road she doesn't remember.

So she stands for the picture,
she looks into the camera,
and lets her attention be the proof
that the photographer was there too,
on that hot, bright road where everything else
washed out to white, chalk and bone.
She is not white.
She is blurred, but not erased,
a restless horse, an untrained rider.
Remember this, she hopes her face can say.
Remember, and when they dig you up again
and say we were mistaken,
tell them it had better be your death
they mean.

# Princess: A Life

*Jane Yolen*

First she is a dreaming dot,
a spot of life in the warm
prison of the womb.

She wakes to a cool world,
a cold curse, a colder kiss,
her own scream.

It is easier to dream.

# Present

## *Nicole Kornher-Stace*

*for Julian*

Now the infection hits the news and Gabriela's mom babysits Jack while Gabriela and her dad go to Wal-Mart for supplies. When it *isn't* the end of the world, her parents are very local-food, free-range, hundred-mile-diet types, but today the Wal-Mart's the only place left open and even Gabriela's mom makes that concession, though she won't set foot inside herself. As Gabriela's dad drives the four miles out of suburbia into town, Gabriela watches the boards go up in people's windows, the padlocks go on doors, the cases of soup cans disappear inside. (Leaving, her dad had grabbed the reusable shopping bags, laughed a little derisive laugh at himself, said Fuck it, and left them in the hall.)

On the way back, the pickup bed and also her lap and footwell full of shopping bags—cans of chili and chickpeas, boxes of cereal, jars upon jars of peanut butter, diapers, multivitamins, cases of ramen, granola, half a dozen can openers—she has a brief panic that they'd get home and the infection would have reached their house already, she'd find her mom gone empty-eyed and gore-mouthed, find Jack lurching instead of toddling. But her dad pulls into the driveway and it's just like when she was a kid, helping him with groceries every Saturday after cartoons, her mom coming out onto the doorstep to help relay stuff to the kitchen, like a fire brigade with pails of water to a burning house. Except now there's Jack perched on her hip, there's a kitchen knife stuck in her belt, and while they rush the bags inside they're watching their neighbors over their shoulders, and their neighbors, rushing bags into their own houses, are watching Gabriela and her parents over theirs.

* * *

Now she wakes up, stretches, says good morning to Jack waking up beside her, and something kicks her in the gut: she remembers what day it is. It's the first day of the future, and the sun comes through the cracks between the two-by-fours across her window, shines down on her futon and Jack's racecar pajamas and the new huge red backpack resting against a bookcase. Her parents each have a backpack just like it upstairs. They packed them together last night. Each one is full of energy bars and Gatorade, a first-aid kit, a flashlight, a pocketknife, pepper spray. Hers also has pull-up diapers and fruit snacks for Jack. Jack has a little backpack himself, and in it he has board books, Matchbox cars, more fruit snacks. Each bag except Jack's has two full bottles of Advil and one of dirt-cheap vodka, in case the time comes and they can't bring themselves to use the knives.

Gabriela's got Jack on the potty and she's already pulling on her yoga pants and sneakers for their morning walk before she remembers morning walks are not happening anymore. She's trying to decide whether she wants to brave taking Jack four doors up the road for playgroup anyway when she hears something upstairs, something like footsteps, something not like footsteps. The not-footsteps approach the basement door, begin descending, slow, uncertain, like whoever it is remembers there being something down here, something worth coming down the stairs for, but couldn't quite remember what it was or why they wanted it to start with. But since she had Jack and moved from her childhood bedroom down to the finished basement where there was room for his stuff, her parents never come downstairs that early in the morning, not when Jack might still be sleeping.

Mom? she says, uncertain.

Then another sound comes from midway up the stairs, a sound like maybe someone gargling mouthwash, only it sounds thicker than mouthwash, and it's like they're trying to talk through it, except that it keeps sloshing out when they try.

For about two seconds she deliberates, hand held out to the door. Then her flight instinct starts firing, that pressure in the small of her back starts shooting through to her navel, her legs start tensing, and the next thing she knows she's got the backpack on one shoulder, Jack hoisted on the other, and she's taking the back door sideways, awkward, and it's hitting her in the ass on her way out, just like the saying says not to.

She's forgotten Jack's backpack, all his board books, Dr. Seuss and *Goodnight Moon* and *The Very Hungry Caterpillar*. She wonders how the hell she's supposed to get him to sleep now.

NOW SHE'S GOT Jack on her shoulders and going as slow as she can along the treeline back of town, staying off the roads, keeping a clear line of sight with the maples at her back. If any of them come up through the woods things'll get interesting, but the town is by far the greater risk, and besides she's faster than they are and she's got Jack as a lookout. They're playing a game called Who Can Be the Quietest. He wins automatically if he sees anyone and pulls her hair to tell her so.

She'd ventured up into town earlier, hugging the back walls of shopping plazas, looking to replenish her stores. She'd only left home two days ago, but Jack was tearing through his fruit snacks like a machine and there was no power in the universe that could get him to swallow so much as one lousy calorie of an energy bar. She'd come around behind the supermarket and found someone's legs hanging out of a dumpster, and the puddle on the concrete strongly suggested the rest of that someone was elsewhere. The delivery door was ajar, streaked at shoulder height with what could have been fingerpaint. She opened the knife, got it in a fist at hip level, took two steps for the door, stopped, looked at Jack, looked around and found nowhere safe to put a wanderlusty three-year-old while she went off to get herself killed over fruit snacks. It did not escape her notice that if this were a movie, this would be the Door the Audience Is Telling the Bimbo Not to Go Through. Well, she's not anybody's goddamn bimbo. Sorry, kid, she murmured, and tousled his hair as best she could with her knife-hand. I promise I won't let you starve.

He's a good kid, her Jack. He didn't throw a tantrum, hungry as he was. Sometimes she even thinks he understands the depth of shit they're in, knows not to make it worse.

They moved on.

NOW SHE'S WALKING beneath the maples and the sunshine and the summer-smell of grass and the roadkill-smell coming off the town, she's walking and she's humming softly to Jack to keep his mind off the sounds in the distance, she's walking and she's thinking about zombie movies again. Thinking how ridiculous it is that they're made to be so *fast*. It doesn't make any sense. She never could figure out why corpses were supposed to suddenly be faster or stronger than they were in life, like some kind of consolation prize for shambling around with your skin plopping off. She's read something about how people only use ten percent of their brains while awake, and it's got her wondering if maybe death—undeath—is supposed to be some kind of loophole that unlocks the other ninety, to let them do ridiculous things like outrun sprinters, chew through walls. She's thinking about it being June, how infections spread faster in the heat, how dead things decompose faster too. She wonders which happens first.

It's not just zombie movies. It's horror stories in general. She remembers back when she first started reading them, huge doorstop anthologies of them that her dad would get at the thrift shop for a dime. She must've been ten or so. They scared her sleepless. One thing she got to noticing in them, though, was how if a story was written in present tense then the protagonist probably survived it, unless there was some kind of twist at the end, but if it was written in past tense then the guy was pretty much screwed.

She's wondering what tense her story's written in. Whether she dies in the dirt with someone's face in her guts. Whether she rides off into the sunset. Whether she wakes up and it was all a dream.

She's wondering where the fuck she's supposed to go before she gets there.

NOW SHE'S TAKEN to calling him Jack the Snack, because she has to convince herself it's funny or she'll go stark raving batshit and there's no coming back from that. The treeline ran out yesterday and she's back among the buildings, old brick townhouses with delis on the corners. There are lots of broken windows on the ground floor, trashed and smeared. There's no glass on the ground. She looks for movement in the windows and sees none. She's so close to breaking down and screaming, hoping the good guys find her first.

The silence is oppressive. The noises are worse. For two days now she's smelled fire but can't find it, fire and a smell like rancid bacon frying. An oily smoke hangs in the air, like what comes out the back door of a diner in July. She's wearing a hole in her shoe. She's cut holes in the backpack, one for each of Jack's legs, and it's a nice hiking backpack so he's pretty stable up there, the backpack strapped around her at chest and waist. His bare toes jostle at her ass with every step.

There are two things that keep her going.

One is Jack's face pressed against the back of her neck. She can't even complain about the way her shoulders cramp in place to carry him, the way she has to stop every half hour and convince him to pee pottyless, the weight of his heavy little butt on her back. The lack of it would weigh much more.

Two is the perverse hope that she'll come across someone she knew in high school, any of the girls who called her Slut or Skank or Maternity Leave when her belly started to round out, any of the boys who'd elbow each other and grin when she walked by, any of the teachers who assumed she was stupid because she'd made one bad call, never mind that she was pulling in the top five percent even through the first trimester when she'd puke til she was dizzy, sit and stare at the wall and wait to die. That weight on her arm again, that face at her shoulder. Bad call? Fuck them. She pictures each of them in turn, maybe pulped into warm jelly by infection, maybe uninfected, healthy, and being torn unceremoniously to bits.

It keeps her going, one foot in front of the other. It keeps her from thinking about her fate. About Jack's. How slow he made her. What would happen when it came to it. Could she let them take him? Could she do it before they got the chance?

You're going to get us killed, kid, she whispers, and he looks up at her uncomprehending, doesn't even know what it means for the mosquitoes when she slaps them off his arms, not really, and he nods at her, all solemnity, fruit snacks on his breath.

NOW SHE'S STANDING in a parking lot over a pair of corpses. No sign of infection on them. Seems that what's done them in is that their throats and most of their abdominal cavities have been emptied out. Last night she wiped the clots off somebody's aluminum baseball bat and now she's holding it at the ready while she toes the larger corpse. The corpse doesn't move. For the millionth time she wonders how it works, the zombie virus or whatever they're calling it on the news now, if there's any news left to call things anything on. She doesn't understand why, when they attack you, there seems to be a magic threshold, on one side of which you get bitten and turn into one of them, on the other side of which you get bitten and die. She's seen a number of them now wounded bad enough they should be dead, they should never have changed to begin with, just went down and stayed down, like these ones. It doesn't even make sense in the movies, what chance does she have to logic it out here?

She doesn't check its pockets. What good will anybody's wallet do her now? There's something clutched in the corpse's hand, though, and when she squats down to get a closer look she sees it's a rosary. She's not sure why she takes it, but she does.

Then there's the smaller corpse. It's not much bigger than Jack. She can't tell if it was a boy or a girl, before. Corpse, she has to use the word corpse, or she'll start wondering what its name was, its favorite color, whether it wanted a puppy, whether it hated macaroni and cheese as much as Jack does.

She glances around. The place is dead empty. Sets Jack down on his feet, just beside her, where a parked car casts a piece of shade on the boiling blacktop. She wonders if the car belonged to the corpses. No key in sight. She starts up a little singsong as she goes to work on the smaller one's shoe. Look at this doll, sweetie, someone got it all messy, you wouldn't make a mess like that, it must have been some *baby,* they're so messy, you're a *big* boy now and you would never.

The other shoe's on the other leg a couple of meters away. She waves the flies off, turns upon the bright green sock a calculating eye. Cold toes, she thinks inanely, and leaves it where it is. Out of the corner of her eye she sees Jack pulling at a stuffed penguin in the corpse's hand. Somehow it's lying in the clear of the worst of the blood. The corpse just won't let go. Me, he shouts at it, annoyed. She bites her lip a second, then kneels and pries the corpse's fist open. Wipes her fingers on her yoga pants and takes his free hand. They stand together, the three of them, looking down.

Say thank you, she whispers.

Thank you, he sings out, and plants a big kiss on the air.

That night, she barricades them in somebody's cellar and reads Jack *Goodnight Moon* from memory, adding in a few extras (goodnight creepy stairs, goodnight dehydration headache, goodnight dead field mouse in the corner, goodnight racecar pajamas that are getting sort of nasty). She keeps adding extras until whatever's happening in the distance stops, it's unlike anything she's ever heard or wants to hear again and she has to keep on talking so he doesn't hear it too, babbling nonsense with her mouth right up to his ear, he's always been so sensitive to others' pain, she can't so much as cut her nails in front of him or else down goes his little brow into little furrows and he's grabbing her hand and kissing it and saying mommy ow, mommy ow.

Still she can't keep talking all night, he needs the sleep and her throat's so very dry. The second she stops he hears it, points toward the wall, toward outside, and asks.

Don't they sound *silly?* she says. Just some people being silly, making silly sounds. Let's snuggle.

And they do.

Once he's asleep, she pulls out the rosary. It smells of blood and cedar and perfume. Her parents are lapsed Catholic, she's only been into a church once and that was for a rummage sale, and she has no idea how to use the thing, feels like a jackass for even framing the notion in those terms, but she finds herself counting the beads of it, one by one, keeping her thumb over the one she's just counted, just how she's teaching Jack to do, so he doesn't count the same thing twice.

As she touches each bead, she's whispering under her breath. It's stupid, she knows it's stupid, it obviously didn't save the woman in the parking lot with the footprints tracking through her guts four feet to either side, but it keeps unspooling out of her, she's blubbering and she can't make it stop. Hail Mary. Hail anybody. I could really use some help here. He's only three and he's run out of pull-ups and I wanted to know what he'd grow up to be. I don't know where my parents are. I think they might be . . . sick. I ran so I could save him. So I could save him from them. I'm running out of water. I don't know where I'm going. Is there anywhere I can go that's better? What will happen to us? I can't kill him don't make me kill him but if it comes to it let him . . . let him go in his sleep, just get him the fuck out of here, they can have me, just get him out, let him find a safe place, don't make him do this. I'm seventeen, I wanted to be a marine biologist, I have a baseball bat and a fucking flashlight and I can't do this, how can I do this, every time I close my eyes I see them pulling him away from me and he's shrieking mommy, all done, mommy, mommy, help, and what am I supposed to do and I can't, I can't, I fucking can't

NOW THEY'VE HIT the farmland outside town, out where she took Jack apple picking last fall, and this time of year the strawberries are fruiting, acres of them, and she can't smell the fires from here, just the hay and the sun and the strawberries and it strikes her for a dizzy moment that the listing world has righted. She steps over the few scraggly rows on the end and sets Jack down in the middle of a clump of berries and they're huge, pristine, untouched, and swollen on the sun. She's found a pistol with three rounds in it and it's jammed down in her waistband and the aluminum bat doesn't leave her swinging hand. She keeps watch. Jack is picking berries and cramming them in with both hands and the juice is running down his chin and then she's down in the rows with him, one eye scanning, one hand picking. She only allows herself a moment. She needs to be alert, not drunk on summer and a bellyful of sugar after days of crumbs. Jack, seeing this, pauses in his cramming to offer up two berries, one in each fist, both bruised with clumsy picking. Eat mommy! he says, red around the mouth and reaching out to her, and her breath hitches in her throat, and she knows that if she were in a movie this'd be Foreshadowing, or the Calm Before the Storm, but then she starts laughing and laughing because she doesn't know what else to do with herself except start screaming and she can't do that, she has to make him believe it's a game or he's going to lose it and then they're done. Anyway it's almost funny. For the first time all week, he looks just like everybody else.

NOW IT'S RAINING, a light sweet twilit summer rain, and she's holed up in the farm stand, and Jack's sleeping on her lap, his hair sticky with strawberry juice, and that's where they find her.

She doesn't know where they came from, how they knew she was there, what they're even doing out so far on the county route, a good ten miles from town, only that she wakes and hears a noise outside, a sort of whistling sigh, which first she takes for wind, except there isn't any. Then she hears something dragging on the gravel of the parking lot, something heavy. And then the doorknob starts to slowly turn, turn and release, turn and release, like it's being fumbled with a slippery hand.

She'd locked it, she knows she'd locked it. Maybe the lock was faulty, maybe Jack had unlocked it when she wasn't looking (though when the hell was she *not looking?*), it doesn't matter. She folds him to her chest and darts in low toward the doorknob, reaches out against all her instinct to flee, tries to turn the lock, but it won't turn, not while the doorknob's turning too.

Jack starts to stir, to knuckle at his sleepy eyes. Still half-asleep, he's going through his wake-up routine, and any minute he'll be peering up into her face, saying boo, mommy! Play?

A low moan rises in her throat. She chokes it back, astonished: she'd sounded just like them. Even as she's ducking and running behind the counter for a chair to wedge beneath the doorknob, some part of her brain is flying out ahead of her, wondering why it is they make such a despairing sound, such a mournful, and what fucking right have they to mourn.

She's got the chair under the doorknob and she's backing, backing. But there are long shadows dragging across all the windows, not only the ones near the door, and now there's something pressed up against the nearest one, something like a stomped windfall plum the size of her face, and from somewhere else she hears the sound of breaking glass, and every drop of blood she owns freezes in that instant into shards.

Awake now, Jack looks up at her and he's got the wide-eyed quivery look he gets at the doctor's office, like if he stays as still and watchful as he can, the nurse with the needle won't know that he's there, and that look scares her even worse than she already is, terrorizes her into moving. She has to get him out. Has to. Failing that, she has to buy enough time to draw the gun and kiss him goodbye and tell him to close his eyes and count to three like she used to do when she had a present for him because if it comes to it, the best present her useless love can give him is an easy death, but in the end, when it does come down to it, can she even give him that?

Well, now or never. She's got him sitting on the counter, facing him into a corner toward a poster of apple varieties so he can't see what's happening at the doors and windows, and she's sliding the safety off down by her hip where he can't see that either. For a second she almost loses her resolve, almost plants one in her temple so she doesn't have to see him die, but leaving him to get eaten even as he clings to her corpse crying wake up mommy, that's the one thing she won't ever do. Give mommy a hug, she tells him, biggest hug you got, and her voice breaks to shit but she can't do much about it, and he flings out his arms and buries his face in her neck and she holds his head there with her off hand while she slips the gun up between them, against his tiny chest, his hammering hummingbird heart, she doesn't even have to aim he's so small, anywhere will do. I love you, sweetie, she whispers into his hair. I'm so fucking sorry.

And suddenly she knows she won't do it. Maybe she knew all along she wouldn't. Couldn't. Can't. She slings him up off the counter, back onto her arm.

They're at the front door. They're at the back door. They're at the side door where the tractors unload the crates of melons in the summer, pumpkins in the fall. But it's at the front window where they've broken through, and she doesn't know if they smell her through the gap or what but they're starting to cluster there, and even as she watches more windfalls appear at the glass, more leave the back wall windows.

Close your eyes, baby, she says, and lunges for the back door.

NOW SHE'S RUNNING, running harder than she's ever run. The evening's still warm, the sunlight slowly bleeding out, and they're still chasing her but they're not quite closing, she's too fast.

For now. She's leaking pretty badly from a long gash down one arm, one cheek is clawed across, her trigger finger broke when one of them grabbed her gun and tore it free, taking the discharged bullet in the eye like a kiss. But what's really got her attention is the place on the front of her shoulder where a plug of flesh has been subtracted. She can't remember what happened there, but the wound is bone-deep and when she stops to dare a look at it, a tiny yellow thing falls tinkling to the road. She picks it up and sobs aloud. A tooth.

How much time does she have? Not enough. Not near enough. She has to get Jack somewhere safe, get far away from him, because they didn't get him, she didn't let them get him, she put her arms, her head, her back between their teeth and him, but when she turns she'll smell the meat on him, and she can't bear to think on that too long. Suddenly, horribly, she knows that when she runs, he won't stay put, he'll follow. That when she turns wrong, turns sick, and comes for him, he won't run, not from her, he'll probably think she's nibbling at his face for tickles before the teeth sink in.

She has to think. She can't. The change is coming on her, the infection nosing through her veins toward her heart, her brain, wherever it is it sinks its roots. She's dizzy. Clammy. Her ears are ringing. She's never been so hungry in her life. Her vision's dimming but her sense of smell is paring to a point and she can read Jack in layers of scent: strawberries, piss-stained racecar jammies, milk-fed flesh, and fear. There's something else there, though, something bittersweet and pungent, with a scorch against her swollen tongue like salt. He loves her. He trusts her. It oozes from his pores. She smells him and she spits and spits until her mouth stops watering.

Her mind's starting to drop down its curtains now, but in one last burst of clarity she sees it like a movie: her and Jack, stumbling down the embankment into the flowering orchard, fleeing the open road, and she knows what happens next. The only chance he has.

She hasn't figured out how the infection works. Maybe nobody ever will. But she's thinking of the corpses lying dead in the parking lot, the not-quite-corpses on her tail, and her brain feels like a soaked sponge in her head, her thoughts go soggy before they quite connect, but she's stumbling down the embankment into the flowering orchard, she's fleeing the open road, she's pushing through the trees to the shed she knows is there from when she took Jack apple-picking a lifetime ago. She'd had to stop and change his diaper and a sunburned woman had directed her down to the shed among the trees. Hope you got wipes, the woman told her, but at least it's a little privacy. Key's above the door.

Key's there now too. She fumbles the padlock, her fingers are so cold. Fights it open. Sets Jack down so she can unfold the knife. Cuts into the back of her hand with the bladepoint, spells FIND. Spells JACK. He watches her wide-eyed, far too scared to cry.

Be brave for mommy, she tells him, kneeling down, her voice slurring to paste. Okay?

Okay, he whispers, and afterward it's all she can do to push him inside and lock the door between them and slip the key where she won't drop it—under her tongue, like a coin—but first she lifts his little arm up to her mouth and bites down hard.

Then she's running back up toward the road, toward them, like the idiot in the movie who Dies That Someone Else Might Live, waving her arms and yelling. Once she's got their attention she takes off down the road, away from him, away from them, and, herd that they are, they follow.

They chase her for a quarter mile before the infection takes her over. It slows her to their speed and they fall in step around her, she disappears among them, like a droplet entering the sea.

* * *

NOW SHE'S GOT something carved into her hand but she can't read it. There's something in her mouth so she spits it out. There's blood on her lips, though, and more blood off back somewhere behind her, she can smell it on the wind, and that's something she can understand.

The thing on the door of the little building is mysterious to her, so she takes it in one hand and pulls until it breaks. The door falls open and there's one like her on the floor, like her only smaller, curled up in a ball and gnawing on a brick. She knows that hunger, knows it deep. The virus has imprinted it upon her every cell. Somewhere even deeper she knows the thing that pulls itself to sitting, blinks up at her with eyes like soft-boiled eggs, and smiles. Boo, mommy! it gurgles around the bolus of its tongue. Mommy play?

She can't carry it anymore, her arm is ruined, but the fires of the town are distant, the others are so near, so strong, and it's been days since it—since he—got down and really walked.

# Old Bone

## *Sandi Leibowitz*

Old Bone come soon

He come while sun too weak to argue
while wind's a scrabble of fingers
'long a banjo skin

Come ashiver in the wheeze of frogs
splutter up from silt and slough
through moss and murk
push past knobby cypress knees
like the river birthin' him

Old Bone slick
Come sliding up slow waters
easy as a gator slicin' duckweed
Even so, he set the hounds to ranting
raise their fur along their backs

He know them old songs
He know them tunes
full o' egrets' white ghost wings
and weepin'

Old Bone, thing he know best
is gaps
—loose fence-slats
chinks in window-frames
that big hollow opened up inside you
since that last gal done drop you

He know how sometimes
you eye them river deeps
thinking maybe down there's better

Old Bone like company
like to tote you down there
join his party in the crawfish mud
chuggin' river brew from gator skulls

Yeah, he know you

Old Bone come soon

# Backbone of the Home

*Lisa M. Bradley*

This was just after the Blackwells and the bank settled
and we'd bought our piece of the old sorghum field.
Your mama and I, we'd cleared the ground
for this house's foundation, and it was one of them
long summer days, so while there was light yet
she ran down with your big brother to the creek
to see if he'd really found a cottonmouth
(no) and I was dealing with the tractor
when I looked up and saw a bent shape,
an old person, creepin' over Half-Moon Ridge.
And for no good reason I could think of
I got a shiver from the top of my head
to my long 'go broken toe.

I went back to work, half-hoping when I looked again
they'd be gone—though that'da been
mighty creepy too—
but next time I checked, I could tell it was a woman,
basket over her arm,
and though rightly I should've gone over
to meet her (or head her off),
I waited til she come up to that old oak,
the one y'all had the rope swing on, 'fore
lightning split it to kindling.
She was whiter than most whites
but dirty, even her dandelion fluff hair
matted with sorghum straw and mud—
least I hoped it was mud—
and the stink on her . . .
it had to be something fierce for me to notice,
considerin' my own hard-won stench.

An apron covered her basket,
the fabric thin and stained, and I
did not like to look on it.

No formalities, she started 'fore I even got my hat off.
"Young man, consider yourself lucky.
You're the first of my visits,
so you'll have first pick
and thus secure your future."
I began to beg pardon,
but she pulled the apron aside
and inside the basket sat nothing but
bones.
Backbones.
Of various shapes and sizes,
too clean to make good soup,
far cleaner than the peddler herself.

When I said we didn't hold with such beliefs
(truth to tell, had never even heard 'em),
she muttered about young'uns
and said, sighin' like,
"You put one beneath your hearth.
It'll grow into the backbone of your home,
even as your spine sits behind your heart."
Now, I did not appreciate her speaking so familiarly
'bout my organs,
but when she pointed
at a bone just smaller than my hand,
like a stone bird with outstretched wings,
I listened, for there was a teacherly quality
in that imperious, if soiled, finger:

"Ox bone if you want your home
solid and strong," she said, "the family,
simple but honest. A pig bone—"
she prodded at one large
as my palm "—for a smaller house,
still sturdy, but your legacy clever and

ruthless. Goose for a cozy nest,
easily repaired, and children who,
though occasionally silly,
take a bird's-eye view. Snake . . . "

Patience straining, I listened to
the rest of her inventory
as manners dictate, but I noticed
one bone went unspoken
and though I wanted nothing more
than to get this woman on her way
(with apologies to our future neighbors)
it's true what your mama says,
'bout your spiteful streak coming from me,
'cuz I couldn't help but gesture at the
overlooked chunk, long as my middle finger.
"If you'll pardon, I think you missed one,"
I said. "What poor animal's that from?"

And the vertical shine that rose
in her watered-down brown eyes,
put me in mind of that cottonmouth
your mama went investigatin'.
"It guarantees ease of body," the witch said—
for that, I'd decided, was what she was.
"Your world built on the backs of others.
Peace of mind from the undying loyalty
of your lineage."
No part of that promise appealed,
so I didn't press, though she'd not quite
answered my question and her head,
tilted to appraise me, sent a second slither
underneath my skin.

"Ma'am," I said, "I can't say we have any use
nor desire for your wares, but I can say
you come 'round here again,
you won't find your reception half so polite."
I only just held back that it'd be

my shotgun did the greeting,
but she cottoned on quick enough and cussed
her way into the distance to hassle
the Vickers and the Cortez sisters
and everybody else who was building
on the old Blackwell property.
I'm grateful to say, however,
I never saw her again, nor
from what I know, did your mama.

Still, I can't say I'm exactly surprised
to hear that old woman visited you today,
new property and all . . .
grateful, though, that you had the good sense
to turn her away—
got that from your mama, I suspect—
and fretful some, to hear that old witch
has collected so many more
of them mystery bones.

# Flap

## *David Sklar*

Tiff and me are skating down the boardwalk toward *Designs on You.* She's finally talked me into getting my wings done. It's scary, you know—they're *sen*sitive—I don't wanna get poked with needles there. Plus, if the colors come out wrong I can't just laser 'em off like the morts do. A wing job is *per*manent.

*Thorn*—if I had Tiffany's wings, I wouldn't let anyone touch 'em, not with a needle or a piercing gun anyway, 'cause she's all *Morpho helena,* you know, so the undersides of her wings are in browns like mine, but with a row of circles from side to side instead of the two big eye spots like I have. But the backs of her wings are a brilliant blue to match her eyes. *Oak*—with colored contacts *and* a glam, I *still* can't get that blue. But Tiff has inscriptions tattooed on the brown side and black tribal patterns across the blue. And then there's the bling—un*e*ven bling, with lapis and amethyst dangling low on the right like a swallowtail, while the left has tiny hoops, all close to the rim, and I'm like, "Can you even *fly,* with all that shit in there?"

She's like, "Who needs to fly?"

I'm like, "I do. Flying *rocks.*"

And she's like, "This is bigger. This is a statement about *me.*" She isn't kidding. She has on a black biker jacket with slits in the back for her wings, held shut at the bottom by the belt, and her hair is chopped short and dyed black, with the tips of it frosted the same burning blue as her wings and eyes. Tiff is all about the statement.

I'm like, "Who cares about making a *state*ment? I want to get up in the air and feel the morning under my wings, with the dew on the tops and the rising sun beneath." The sound of the ocean to our left lends its breath to my words.

And she's like, "Yeah, whatev. And if one of the morts looks up?"

"I put on a glam before I go, all he sees is a sparrow."

"I don't do glams."

"WHAT?"

"No glams. Just me. What you see is what you get."

"You're a freak."

"Right on."

"Not even to hide your wings?"

"*Ash,* Heather, the morts are loopy. A chick with wings doesn't faze 'em—they think it's a fashion statement I picked up in a store."

"Whatev."

"Glams strip your focus, Heather; they waste your spark making lies."

Just then a crouching junkie tugs on my skirt and asks for spare change. I fan myself to a stop and I get on one knee to see her face. As Tiff does a loop around, I brush my fingers along the kid's temple and imbue her with the softest glimmer of the edge of a dream.

"Thank you," she barely whispers, with gentle ecstasy in her eyes.

But Tiff, she's all like, "Wha'dyou do that for?"

"What?"

"Di'nt you *hear* what I just said?"

"Whatev."

"This is *serious,* Heather. Don't waste your spark."

"Whatever. We're almost there."

"Do it once and they'll all want it," Tiffany says, and she skates away.

I skate after her. But just before I do, I see a man standing just off the boardwalk, watching us, with a malevolent hunger in his eyes.

*DESIGNS ON YOU* is right off the boardwalk, a little stall fronted by two big double doors shaped like big patterned wings, with eye spots like mine but in*tense,* bronze circles inside emerald green, ringed by deep purple around the rims.

Tiff opens the door and skates in, saying "Hey Gwyd," totally caz, but me, I've never been in there before. The place has sketches up and down the walls, black work and knotwork, animals and heroes. There's a drawing of a claymore, big as life, with a black filigree down the silver blade. I wonder how tall you'd have to be to wear a picture that big on your leg.

A muscled guy with silver-tipped antlers inlaid with turquoise sees us skate in. His tank top shows off the coiled black tats on his arms. A chunk of amber hangs from his neck with a tiny man inside. "So you're Heather?" he asks.

"Uh—yeah."

"I'm Gwydion. This is my shop. Heard a lot about you." He gives me an unshaven smile that melts me cold, and then he continues, "Let's get to work."

So he gets out his sketch pad and colored pencils, and starts talking me through my wings as he draws them in. "This is a classic pattern, the death's head moth, and there's a lot of inspiration to be had—just look at my doors. I mean, the basic pattern is gorgeous, just gorgeous, in sepia and tan, but if you add a touch of jade for accent here . . ." and as he says this he picks up a pale green pencil and shades over the rim of the tan inside where he's drawn my wing on the page.

I gasp, because it really *is* beautiful, and until this moment I thought I could back out, but now that I've seen his sketches I know I gotta see it through. I bite my lip and nod. I'm already imagining the pain.

And he can see it in my face, because he puts the pencils down without drawing anything else, and says, "Let's start with that, and then see how we feel."

IT TEARS. IT *tears.* The pain is furious and bright. I clutch Gwydion's other hand as the needle sears into my wing. I cling to the sound of the ocean outside, to the passing voices. A radio wanders by, giving voice to a song that is nothing but screech. I cling to that.

The tattoo shop is lit by small strings of lights and some old but powerful lamps. Tiff is standing at a counter in the center of the room, idly picking up knickknacks and looking at them while Gwydion does his work. I search for solace in the mesmeric pattern of Tiffany's blue-and-black wings, but all I can think of is how did she sit through that, when I al*ready* want to crawl under the counter and weep. He's barely started, and I've suffered a lifetime of pain.

In the shop, across the room, a radio predicts rain. "You know, that used to be all us," I hear Gwydion say, through a dream of pain. No, scratch—the pain is real, but everything else is a dream. I am whimpering, trying to hold it in, but he just keeps talking, "Mortal man *took* it from us—assigned causes and made observations to lock them in. Now if we want it back we gotta put our own stamp on the wind, the rain, the earthquakes—"

Tiff laughs, a *pffthy* laugh. "Earthquakes?" she says. "Where you gonna find a glam big enough to cover dancing giants in Southern Cal?"

"I have other ideas," says Gwyd. But before he can say what, a gaunt and shivering mort walks in and looks straight at me. He says, "You gotta give me what you gave my friend."

I stare at him for a moment before I recognize the hungry man from just off the path.

Gwydion sets down the needle. Cool relief on my wing, and my back untenses.

"You gotta," the mort repeats.

Gwyd steps forward. "Sir, you are in my place of business and I will have to ask you to leave."

"I need what you gave Jenny," he says, stepping closer to me.

Gwydion continues to walk forward and puts his right hand on the mort's wrist. "Sir, you are—"

"I don't *CARE!*" And the skinny mort tries to shake Gwydion's hand off his wrist, but Gwydion doesn't let go, and before you know it, Gwyd has a silver claymore in his left. I didn't see where it came from, but the big picture of the sword is now a blank paper on the wall. Then the mort pulls a gun on Gwydion and says, "You got that, I got this—y'wanna see who's faster?" And Gwydion lets go his wrist and steps back a step.

And I think, *No good to anyone,* but as the junkie repeats "I need her to give me—" Tiff shouts "ENOUGH!"

And I didn't realize until that moment she had *bane-sidhe* blood, but the edge in her voice holds us pinned in our places. As the lingering sound of her shimmers aloud in the air, she moves her wings. Slowly at first, and the runes and patterns inscribed on the membrane delve into their inner workings . . . the power collects around the jewels that hang from her right wing . . . they start to turn . . . then the wind rises up in the room and all the pictures pinned to the wall respond to the breeze as it moves wid'shins around the studio, flapping the paper, and she fans it on.

I'm frightened for her, I really am, but what's happening in the pictures grabs my attention and won't let go. Strange birds and Chinese unicorns look up and then duck for cover from the wind that portends the storm about to come. A dragon stretches, languid with anticipation.

"What's she doing?" the junkie shouts and points the trembling gun at her, but by now Tiff has found her power and is beating her wings so strong that the drawings are flying around the room. My skates are slipping out under my chair, and I have to hang on to the counter to keep from getting swept away.

"Make it stop!" the mort shouts at her. By now the tattoo needles are rattling in their stands, and the colored pencils are rolling around on the table.

There is a muffled sound like thunder and I realize the gun has fired, and Gwydion swings the claymore much too late. The bullet struggles across the wind, but the anticlockwise gale beats down the force of its forward momentum, and the bullet slows . . . almost stops . . . then spins round the room wid'shins in Tiffany's orbit and comes around to nail the shooter in the fleshy part of the hand, below his thumb. The colored pencils go next and stab his arm, and then the needles impale him between the bones of his forearm, sending the pistol clatterspinning to the floor and knocking his wrist just out of the way of Gwydion's sword.

The shivering junkie stumbles backwards out of the shop into the light, his arm impaled several times through. Tiffany comes back to herself, and the winds die down. The scattered pages settle into a heap in one corner, and the creatures in the pictures seem to huddle together for solace.

"Excuse me. I have to retrieve my instruments," Gwydion says, and he steps outside, silhouetted against bright sun. I stare on, stunned.

"Don't worry," Tiff tells me, as the first in a series of low, wracked screams comes in the door. "He'll sterilize everything before he uses it again."

And I stare at Tiffany's wings and I realize what she has done, how she has stunted herself for power over wind. How the imbalance that keeps her grounded lets her whip up a cyclone around her when she must. I *have* to fly, but right now I'm fluttering inside so bad I can't even muster the glam I need to keep the morts from seeing me as me. So I cower in my chair and slowly flap, flap, flap until the tremor of my fearful heart subsides.

# Rhythm of Hoof and Cry

*S. Brackett Robertson*

She didn't worry at the first appearance of the horns,
small buds, nearly flush with his skull.
She assumed all men must grow them, when they're thirty
She'd forgotten he was human.

He was less certain about them, peaking above the crown of his head
but he was in her country now,
living behind the wall of thorns.
He'd been cut and bruised when he crossed, but that was a year ago.

He didn't tell her of his dreams, of the cold air and the restless bodies
and the urge to flee
he didn't tell her about the hounds.
He was afraid, when he awoke, but he told himself these things are
usual here

Once they grew longer, started to show at the top of his shadow, she
wondered,
quietly, how he was adjusting. The air was different here, and the water
he'd never drunk it before for fear of entrapment.
He said he was still, said he was calm, but he crossed the brambles
She'd seen his cuts. She'd seen the fear in his eyes when he awoke.

She heard the hounds when he rose from his bed,
moonlight gleaming on his horns, now reaching curved to the moon
when he looked towards her, it was with emptied eyes,
he startled when she reached towards him, and fled.

# The Silver Comb

*Mari Ness*

I know, oh how, oh how I know
what happens to those who yield,
who bend to touch the silver combs,
and find themselves dragged beneath the cold grey hills,
drowned beneath the banshee's touch.
I know of the men who have died beneath
those silver breasts and shining hair,
or turned into nothing but scattered dust
as they sat enthralled by haunted song,
by fiddles and harps carved from sheer moonlight,
by the deadly sweetness of silver lips.

And I am to wed tomorrow eve,
the son of the lord with the rough fists
and ready smile, who waits even now
to tumble me into a bed of fine straw
and fill me with fine children.

But oh, the comb gleams in the silver moonlight,
and oh, the song is very sweet!

And oh, she shines in the grey moonlight,
and the wisps of fog rise up to greet her.
And oh, her voice calls, rich with promised honey,
hot with the warmth of crackling fires.

It would not take much to stroke that comb,
to fall beneath the banshee's lips.
I imagine myself sucking at her breasts,
and I bend, I bend to the road.

# Milkweed

## *Cedar Sanderson*

Cecelia sat on her horse, skirts and kirtle hiked up around her knees. She was staring in dismay at the field before her. That winter when Hugh had bought it, it was a smooth expanse of white, looking just as a hayfield ought. No brush or weeds pushing up through the snow, and Hugh had said he recalled it was mowed twice yearly. She could expect a couple of tons of good hay. Only now she saw the fraud that had been sold to them.

She dismounted stiffly. She rarely rode anymore; most of her time was spent in the gardens and house these days. With two young daughters, her world had slowly telescoped inward until the walls were pressing in on her. Today she had been eager to get out, into the fresh spring air, to ride and enjoy the warm sun. Now, her heart was falling as she walked into the field.

The grass was eclipsed by the unmistakable shoots of milkweed that were already twice the height of the green blades. She touched one, feeling the velvety texture of the furled leaves. The entire field was full of it. Worthless . . . She sighed deeply, her hand falling back to her side and clenching on a handful of her skirt. In order to make this back into a hayfield every stalk of it would have to be hand-pulled. The roots were persistent, too deep to plow out, and brittle. Every broken bit would throw up new plants.

"Oh, I could just cry!" Cecelia exclaimed to the blue sky overhead. It wouldn't cripple them, but the family couldn't afford to throw money away. And it would disappoint her husband.

"Please don't." A sweet voice responded.

Startled, Cecelia looked around. She didn't see anyone there.

"Look down." The voice commanded with a ring of amusement.

The tall woman looked down at the grass and milkweed, and saw a tiny person standing on the tip of one of the shoots. Cecelia sank to her knees slowly, her heart pounding. She knew this was one of the Faeries, and to offend them was to court death, or worse.

"Greetings, Lady." A court bow was difficult on one's knees, but she assayed it to try and appease the tiny magical being. A trill of laughter and a returned bow rewarded her.

"Merry meet, Cecelia duLac."

Cecelia saw a shimmering pair of wings flick out, and then the Faery was hovering for a second, before she grew bigger. Cecelia blinked, and the other was standing nose to nose with her, waist high had she been standing.

"I am Eudica, queen of the Lac Faery clan." The royal Faery introduced herself to the human kneeling before her.

"I am flattered to meet you, my lady. You know me?" The farm wife was dismayed at the thought of magic in her safe little world. Nothing good came out of meddling with magic.

"I knew who this field was bought for."

Cecelia looked around. "What is it that makes you interested in this?" She heard the disdain in her own tone and blushed. She was speaking far too directly to a being who could destroy her, however delicate the queen appeared. "No good hay will come from here for two years at least."

Eudica shook her head. "I am interested in the milkweed." Mirroring Cecilia's earlier gesture, she petted the fuzzy stalk nearest her.

Cecelia blinked. "Why?" she blurted.

"I have my reasons." The queen replied demurely, but Cecelia saw a twinkle in her eye.

Emboldened by that, the farmwife in Cecelia rose to the surface and she began to negotiate. "What about my hay, then? The sheep need to eat all winter, and I will have to buy another hayfield."

Eudica laughed. The silvery trill made Cecelia smile despite her trepidation. She knew now why people became so enchanted with Faeries they would do anything to see one again. The little queen stretched her wings out, looking over the field. Cecelia recognized deep thought and remained silent, looking around herself, enjoying the warm spring sun. Behind her, the shaggy horse delicately grazed around the milkweed stalks. He knew not to eat them.

The air smelled sweet from the flowers in the hedgerow. She noted the apple blossoms and made a mental note to return for the fruit in late summer. Wild apples added a nice tartness to cider. In the corner of the field, a massive oak towered, its leaves only just starting to come out. Oaks always came last to spring.

Eudica pointed at it. "Dig under that tree and you'll have your answer."

Cecelia looked at her in surprise. "Dig under the tree?"

"Yes, Farmwife. I do pay my rents, in more than Faerie gold."

Cecelia winced. That was a nasty trick some humans had gotten the worse from, gold that vanished as soon as the bargain was fulfilled. She wondered who had been at fault, though, looking at Eudica and seeing the honesty in the Faery's eyes. Humans were every bit as treacherous and deceitful as the stories made Faeries out to be. Hugh had told her often enough that her judgement of a person was what he'd rely on to death, and for once, she decided to follow his advice. Her assessment of the queen was that she could be trusted, at least in this matter. Add to that, she'd just as soon not offend the powerful being.

"Done. I will rent you the field, and the milkweed, in return for what is buried beneath the tree." Hesitantly, she held out her hand to the queen. Eudica took her fingertips in both velvety hands. Cecelia looked down at their hands, the queen's fingers like a baby's, contrasting with her own reddened, rough ones.

"You will not be sorry, Cecelia. I like you, farmwife, you are refreshingly direct and honest."

Cecelia felt her cheeks warm. "I have had no dealings with the Land of Faerie. I can but behave as I am."

"High court is ever a maze of manners and dangers." Eudica sighed. "Would I had more dealings with farmwives."

Cecelia felt a surprising twinge of pity for the queen. She was lonely, she realized. "Perhaps we shall meet again."

"Oh, certainly we shall!" Eudica laughed again, and as she did that small enchantment, she shrank to the shimmering sprite she had been when Cecelia first saw her. "Good day, Farmwife!" she called as she flew away.

She would have to return with tools; she had nothing but her hands to dig with. Cecelia went to the horse and hoisted herself back into the saddle, rearranging her skirts for decency. How she was going to explain to Hugh that a Faery queen was renting the hayfield, she had no idea.

On the following morning, she returned with mattock and axe for roots and let the horse free to graze again. She had come alone to do this, as she had no idea what she would find. Walking under the wide branches, she saw immediately where she would need to dig, a patch of disturbed, weedy ground. An hour later, dirty and hot, she stared into the hole and was reminded that Faerie was not only a realm of beauty, but of fierce, proud creatures. The man had died of a crushed skull, that was immediately obvious. She wondered what he had done to deserve a lonely burial, with the leather bag carefully placed on his chest. Without looking, she knew it would be filled with gold coins.

She knew of none who would be lying here, and she knew everyone in the surrounding countryside. As Hugh's wife, it was her role to know and tend those who were ill or struck down. This man had been here for no longer than a few years, or his bones would be darker. She had seen an old grave dug up, as a child, and she remembered the bones of the consecrated grave, teak-dark like the deck of a ship. This unconsecrated grave with its tumbled bones was the work of the Faeries, and she shivered as she reached for the bag.

Reluctantly, she lifted it out, feeling the weight of it, and began to rebury the body. The queen had indeed paid her rent in real gold, in a macabre way that reminded Cecelia to be careful in her dealings. She rode home, shivering once in a while despite the heat of the sun.

Cecelia did not return to the field for months, until late summer. She rode slowly there, clinging to the cantle with both hands and letting the horse make his own way down the lane. She had fought for this time in the sun, pleading to be allowed out of sight of her protective family. The horse, his coat sleek now rather than the winter shaggy of spring, stopped at the newly built gate to the field and she slid down. Once on the ground she stood for a second on wobbly legs, then reached out to the gatepost for support. Perhaps it was a mistake to come this far so soon.

She wasn't sure why she had come here, only that after her illness the thought of seeing and smelling the milkweed blossoms had called to her. The field was almost unrecognizable, the thickest crop of milkweed she had ever seen, the air thick with the spicy scent of the blossoms. The purple globes of blossoms held waist-high to her made her press a hand to her belly, then sink slowly to the ground, leaning against the post, lost in thought.

Eudica fluttered to her knee, surprising Cecelia. She had not expected to meet the queen here. Much less to have the powerful being greet her so intimately. The sprite shimmered, and then grew to child-size. She wrapped her arms around Cecelia, and the farmwife burst into tears. She was embarrassed to do this in front of the Faery, but she had not cried a tear since her loss. Now, it seemed, she would not be able to stop again.

"Shh . . . There, now." Eudica stroked her hair and cheek softly. "Tell me what has befallen you, my dear Farmwife."

Cecelia hiccuped and drew a deep breath. "I lost a child." She pressed her hand to her belly again. It felt concave, after the few short months of life growing there, the firm curve that had held a child. Her eyes filled with tears again, and her chest hurt both from the tears and the pain she had been in since the night she knew her baby was dead.

"Oh, my dear." Eudica hugged her again, and then sat on the ground next to her. "Tell me about it."

"I know how fragile life is, and how few of us mortals live to be old. But the babies . . . I have always feared losing one, you know. My daughters I carried safely, this son . . . I lost. They tell me not to fret so, that there will be another child." Her voice grew higher as she spoke, and she took deep breaths, trying not to let hysteria overwhelm her.

"We of Faerie understand how precious each child is. We have so few . . ." Eudica's voice trailed off, and Cecelia heard the sorrow in the other woman's broken sigh. Now it was her turn to reach for the Faery's hand, taking it gently.

Her heaviness of heart kept her from speaking, and finally Eudica looked her in her eyes. "I could bring you a child."

Horrified, Cecelia drew her hand back. "Some other mother's grief to be my profit? A changeling in her nursery so that I may give my husband a son? No . . . No!"

The Faery Queen smiled at her. "That answer was from the heart. You are a good woman, Cecelia. Some of us . . . of my people, are not so honorable as you. I have never taken a human child to keep. I would not bring you one."

"You were testing me again." Cecelia sighed. "We share this, then, my lady. We are mothers, first, no matter whether human or Faery. And the children are so dear."

Eudica smiled sweetly. "Mothers are the same the world around. Call me Dicey, my friend, and I shall feel at ease."

Cecelia tried to smile back, her heart lighter for the tears shed and pain shared. "And I am Celia, to my friends. The milkweed grows so well, I hope it is meeting your needs."

She hoped to change the subject to something less painful, and stop her tears. The Faery must have understood, for she smiled as she responded.

"Oh, it is. Look . . ." Dicey stood and took a few steps into the milkweed, almost disappearing in the plants that were as tall as she was. She returned with a fat striped caterpillar in her hands and set it on Celia's palm. It reared up and twisted around, then marched stolidly toward the now distant vegetation it wanted. Celia laughed.

"It tickles, all the little feet. These grow into monarch butterflies? And they are your livestock, aren't they?"

She looked up at Dicey, smiling through the tears on her cheeks. The antics of the little insect, trying to get home again, had cheered her irrationally. She felt good here. Warm for the first time in a long while. She had been so cold, from the loss of blood and despair. Even the sunshine hadn't helped. The loneliness had been from the women around her making it feel as though she was wrong in being sad about the loss of her child.

"They are like horses, you see." Dicey sat back down and patted the caterpillar, which was now making its way down Celia's skirt. "When they migrate south, we go with them, our carriages woven from milkweed silk and pulled by butterflies."

"But you fly yourself."

"Yes, but that long it is too tiring, you see. And our babies cannot fly. Nor can we stay here, under the snow, without starving and freezing."

Celia nodded. It made sense to her, and she realized what a great secret she had just been entrusted with. She carefully lifted the caterpillar and set it on a nearby milkweed leaf. It immediately began to eat. She sighed.

"The field will be safe with me," Celia promised.

"I know it will." Dicey sat next to her, her head against Celia's shoulder. They both drowsed in the summer sun, listening to the hum of bees in the milkweed and intoxicated by the scent of the flowers.

Finally the queen sighed and murmured, “I have not had peace like this in years, my friend.”

“Nor I, work is always demanding my attention, if not the children.”

“You said you have two daughters?”

Celia had not said, but she was grateful both for the queen’s observation of her family and the opportunity to talk about them. “Elspeth and Jane . . . they are becoming beautiful young ladies.”

“Accomplished with spinning and weaving, I imagine. I know their mother is.”

Celia looked at her in surprise. “How do you know?”

“In the marketplace your cloth is sought after, and your dear husband speaks very highly of you.”

Celia boggled a little at the idea of solid, quiet Hugh speaking to the Faery Queen. Dicey laughed for the first time that day.

“I am not always seen by humans while I listen, my dear. How did you explain this . . .” she gestured at the field, “to him?”

“I told him I was going to try spinning milkweed silk from the seed pods.”

“Oh . . . Hm. Would that work for you?”

Celia shook her head. “I tried it as a girl. The strands are too thin and fragile, even the lightest touch of a spinner will break the strands.”

Dicey nodded. “Our carriages are spun by Faery hands, so much different than your spinning wheel and mortal fingers.”

Celia smiled. “There is not much of magic in my world.”

“I would give you a gift, then, with no expectation of anything in return. Magic and happiness you need in your life. This fall, gather the pods, with your daughters, just as they brown, but before they split open. Try to spin the floss and see what comes of it.”

Celia heard hoofs, then and turned to look up the lane to see who was coming. Dicey shrank to sprite size and kissed Celia’s ear quickly.

“See you in the spring . . .” Celia heard as she flew away. Hugh was riding up the lane toward her. He looked concerned that she was leaning against the post. As he neared her he slid from the horse’s back and hurried to her.

“Are you hurt?” he exclaimed, dropping to his knees and running his hands over her.

Celia laughed at his tender concern. "No, only resting in the warmth. Sit with me a minute? Then we will go home."

He took the spot at her side where Dicey had been just before. She snuggled into his strong shoulder.

"Isn't it pretty?"

"Yes, and it has put the roses back in my good wife's cheeks, so I am grateful even for a field of weeds."

"It's a special place." She murmured to him, glad he loved her enough to accept an oddity. He put an arm around her and held her close in silence for a while.

"I am glad to see your grieving abate," he said finally. "I wanted to ask you . . ."

"Yes?" She looked up into his grave face.

"Was it because you thought I wanted a son?"

"No . . . well, yes, that too."

He hugged her. "All I want is you, safe, and our two living children are blessings. Never think I would endanger you simply for an heir. My nephew is a grand boy, and he will do admirably."

Celia sniffled a little into the linen waistcoat she had spun, dyed, woven, and sewn herself for him. "I lost our child . . ." she cried.

"I know. I wanted him, too, for all he might have been. I am just glad you are safe, today. We will never forget him."

She nodded, too overwhelmed for words. He was a good man, her husband.

"Come, Wife." He lifted her gently to her feet. "Can you ride?"

"I think so. Resting has done me good."

"Then perhaps I will bring you back again. Tonight, though, I am hungry and would carry you home and feed you."

Celia surprised herself with a giggle. He helped her onto the horse and they rode companionably back to the farmhouse talking of mundane things such as crops and the children.

In the fall when she and the children harvested the milkweed pods, the wind laughed and rattled among the dry stalks, as if a gang of Faery children played at their sides. Celia, strong and hearty again, took the time to sing and play with her daughters as they worked. That night, in the firelight because she was too impatient to wait for morning, she spun floss that shone like a pearl in the ruddy light, whiter and finer than linen ever was, as fine as the Orient silk she had once seen. It was strong, too. She could not break it however hard she pulled.

Celia sat at her spinning wheel and laughed in delight. The Faery's gift would be worn by human kings, she had no doubt, and Hugh would be even more puffed up about his wife in the market-place. But at this moment, all the farmwife wanted was for spring to come, and the return of her good friend, the Faery Queen.

# Never Told

## *Jane Yolen*

The story of it, the once upon a time
knitting nettle shirts, fingers on spindles,
climbing down a golden rope of hair,
waking up in a coffin of glass—
and you have to ask yourself is it worth
stung and pricked fingers, broken teeth,
shorn head, frothy cough
of poisoned apple into your skirt?
This is the part of the tale never told.

The story of it, the happy ever after,
when the ball is over, sleep is done,
slipper fits, beast becomes man,
witch is shoved in the oven,
giant craters below the stalk—
is it worth the pain when the prince cheats,
the man is a beast, the foot grows fat,
the witch's children take you to court,
the giant's seed kudzus the farm.
That is the other part of the tale never told.

# Foxfeast

*Yoon Ha Lee*

There's nothing in it for foxes.

Your merry eyes,
your marrow sweet as abrasions,
the machined curve of your thigh.

The broth of your blood.
Your breath like slow roses.

Foxes do not seek your face
in the hundred hunched windows
of starwheel towers.

Foxes do not take by force
the hinges of your on-off heart,
the stuttering tears.

Their prey lives in paradox wires.
Broken alleys. Penrose tile wars.

Foxes have already gnawed
your icemoon cities, knotted
your lightships fast.

Now, when they feast,
smiling their entropy smiles,
they chew the axioms first.

# Seeds

## *Beth Cato*

the young girl filled her pockets with dirt of the field
let it warm against her hips on the long drive home

home, where Mama fussed and hollered, and sisters cried
her bedtime lullaby of gunshots and squealing tires

from the apartment trash she unearthed two old mason jars
her fingers shoveled the soil within

she set the jars on the sill that faced morning
inside, she planted her two favorite plastic horses

ones named Black Beauty and Mr. Bojangles
purchased at the dollar store at First and Ivy

she watered them with a lipstick-stained Dixie cup
nestled her chin on her forearms, and waited

hours and weeks and forevers of school days
Mama's door slams rattling bones and jars

until hard hooves broke through crusted dirt
danced in small circles within her soft palm

to her joy, they smelled of mud and greenery on the wind
MADE IN CHINA still imprinted on inner hind legs

she shared with them her favorite Cheetoes and Pepsi
so like her, they'd grow up big and strong

so strong, that someday they'd bust down that door
gallop down the stairs and those tight city streets

in search of the dirt from which they were born
where car tires whisper and crickets chirp in verse

# Seedpaper

## *Rhonda Parrish*

Rosalie lived in a stone cottage at the edge of the woods. She had a little walled-in garden at the back of her house that was an immense source of mystery for the children of the nearby village, as was she. No one knew where she'd come from. Unlike everyone else, whose families had lived in the area since time immemorial, she had just shown up one day, asking about the little cottage, and then paying Old Mr. Boucher his asking price in cash.

She endeared herself to the villagers by hiring all the local craftsmen to furnish her new home. Carvers, the blacksmith, potters and weavers—she sought all their skills out and paid them very well.

She also arranged for an unusual contraption to be made for her. It was meant, she said, to help her create paper on which to record her stories because, when you got down to the marrow of it, she was a storyteller. She created her own paper, beautiful stuff that was strung through with coloured fibers and peppered with seeds and blossoms. She wrote on it, her hand as elaborate as the paper and reminiscent of medieval scribes. She would often sew the pages together, creating books that she lined up, spines out, along her mantle. Sometimes though, she'd bury them by moonlight in her garden—and what a garden it was!

It was a riotous place where squash shared space with tomatoes and daisies while morning glory threaded its way around everything and poppies painted random splashes of red among the greenery. Her vegetables were renowned in the towns nearby for their purity of flavor.

Being invited to dine at her home was an enviable privilege and the meal itself often compared to a religious experience. After dining with her the shopkeeper adjusted his scales to be more accurate and dear Mrs. Gagnon—who everyone knew to be an alcoholic—found the strength to give up the bottle.

One day Joseph, the blacksmith, was working in the forge attached to his house. The furnace had been put out, but the room had yet to let go of its heat, and sweat covered him like an extra layer between him and his clothes while he swept up and prepared to retire for the night.

"Mr. Roy," Rosalie said. Her voice was as soft as dandelion fluff but still audible over the clink and clunk of his tools as he put them away.

"Ma'am," he replied and tipped an imaginary hat in her direction.

"I was wondering if you'd like to join me for dinner tomorrow."

"I—" the big man began, but was interrupted by his sons, Pierre and François, popping up like gophers from behind the half wall that divided the forge. There had been a fire last winter and he still hadn't completed all the repairs. The boy's impish faces, identical to any who didn't know them, glowed with glee, and their flaxen curls bounced with each movement.

"Would we?" they cried in unison and then tumbled into the forge proper, flowing off one another in their excitement. Soon they arranged themselves, one on either side of their father. He looked down at them, and then ruffled their hair with his blackened hands. "Little scamps, what were you doing back there?"

"Playing spies!" Pierre answered.

François added, "We saw you scratch your—" and then, looking over at their visitor, he fell silent.

"I think," the blacksmith said with a chuckle, "we would be honored to join you."

The boys shouted their excitement.

"I'll see you tomorrow then," Rosalie said, tucking a long strand of raven hair behind her ear and backing out the door into the purple twilight.

After she was gone, Joseph smacked the boys on their bottoms, "All right, go and tell Miss Marie we'll be going out for dinner tomorrow and that I'll be right in."

Ever since the blacksmith's wife had died, swept away by the river the spring before, Marie Leclerc had been taking care of the boys, the house and their meals. Joseph paid her as well as he could but everyone knew she did it for the children. She loved them as though they were her own, and they were the nearest she'd ever come to having any.

The next day Joseph finished his work early and scrubbed his hands as best he could though the valleys in the pads of his fingers and the palms of his hands were perpetually black. The boys were dressed in their Sunday best and Marie had washed them until they squeaked.

The blacksmith's shop crouched at the edge of the village, so it was an easy walk to Rosalie's. The boys burbled with excitement and kicked up grey dust on the road that clung to their trouser cuffs like lichen on a rock. Joseph, loathe to dampen their mood, didn't try to restrain them.

Before they reached the cabin they could see Rosalie silhouetted in the doorway, clutching the fingers of one hand in the other. At the sight of her the boys picked up speed and, whooping and hollering, arrived at her home a tumble of limbs and curls. She welcomed the children in, and by the time Joseph arrived and doffed his cap, the boys were out in the back garden playing.

While Rosalie put the finishing touches on dinner, Joseph watched her. She moved in a way that suggested if he were to make a loud noise she'd jump out of her skin. She was an attractive woman with fine features and long black hair. She was young enough for it to be unlikely she was a widow, yet old enough it would be odd for her to not have been married. She glanced over at him and half-smiled. He blushed at being caught and turned to look casually around the cottage.

It was small, one room with a ladder up to a loft bedroom. The kitchen took up half of it, and its table dominated it. The remainder of the room was a sitting area with a fireplace on the west wall. Out the window overlooking the famous garden, the blacksmith could see the peaked roof of the outhouse to the left of the garden's stone wall.

Returning his attention indoors, Joseph's gaze fell on the long line of books spanning the mantle, and he let his breath out through his teeth. "Did you write these, Miss Rosalie?"

"I did," she said with a smile that didn't reach her eyes.

"There looks to be as many books here as there are families in the village."

"Very near," she said, laughing nervously.

"I never learned to read," Joseph said, taking a place at the table and watching her move about the stove and counter. "Learned my numbers, but always knew I'd take the forge over from my pa, so learning to read seemed a path to pride."

"My stories aren't meant to be prideful," she said. After a thoughtful pause she continued, "They are meant to enlighten. Sometimes all people need to change things, to make them better, is a little enlightenment."

Joseph smiled and muttered in agreement. Then he leaned over to inhale the scent of the paper-like poppies which sat, in a milk bottle vase, in the middle of the table. In a blink, instead of seeing the flower's red petals he was kneeling beside the river looking down at his wife. Her cornflower eyes, wide open beneath the water, stared up at him while the current played with her blonde hair, caressing it like a lover.

Then he was back in the cottage.

His heart raced like a deer in his chest and, fearful of what look might be on his face, his eyes jumped toward Rosalie. She'd left the stove and was at the garden door with her back to him calling the boys in for dinner. He ran a callused hand down his face, from his forehead to his chin, and then forged a smile out of his features. That was what he presented to Rosalie and the boys as they bounded into the cabin, filling it with their exuberance.

"I grow them in my garden," Rosalie said, gesturing toward the flowers. "Poppies are one of my favorites. Their seeds are small enough that they are easy to work into the paper, and their colors are nice too. Those ones grew from a story."

"They are pretty exceptional," Joseph said.

"I don't plant all my stories," Rosalie said, moving about the kitchen and dishing up dinner while the boys took their places at the table. "Only the special ones."

Pierre leaned over to smell the flowers and Joseph very nearly put a hand out to stop him but was saved the risk of looking foolish when Rosalie swooped in, picked up the vase and replaced it with a bread bowl.

"Aw, I wanted to smell," Pierre whined.

Rosalie set the vase on her windowsill beside a bunch of daisies. Picking out one of the white flowers with butter-yellow centers she handed it to Pierre. Her fingers shook slightly and the movement was amplified in the petals of the bloom. "Smell that one, it's even nicer."

"Mmm," he said, grinning. "It smells like Mama's perfume."

"Lemme smell!" François said, nudging his brother and thrusting his face toward the blossom. Inhaling deeply he slumped back into his chair with a smile. "Nah, it smells like her sugar pie."

"Does not!"

"Does too!"

"You know," Rosalie said, "some people say poppies and daisies don't have a scent, but I think they smell different for everyone."

The boys looked at one another and nodded as though that had been their position the entire time, and Joseph breathed a sigh of relief.

"And that's why—" Rosalie continued, setting a bowl in front of each of the boys. Pierre's slopped a little gravy onto the table which she quickly wiped up with the corner of her apron. "—we will each get a dinner a little different from everyone else's. We'll each have one vegetable no one else does. Pierre and François, you get celery in your stew, I will have broccoli, and your father can have carrots."

The boys frowned down at their bowls while Rosalie dished out dinner for herself and Joseph, but she laughed. She set the blacksmith's bowl before him and took a seat at his side with her own dinner, then said, "Trust me. You'll like it."

The boys' doubts about dinner evaporated like dew in sunshine as they swallowed the first mouthful. Their gazes turned inward and as they took another spoonful to their lips François began to hum *V'là l'bon vent.*

They'd tucked into a barn-raising they could usually only recall as a collection of impressions. A hint of sawdust, an echo of a fiddle. Now, however, they were right there, reliving it as though it were happening for the first time. It was their first time out since the fire that had claimed half the forge and made the smoke which stole their sister's breath and her life with it.

The air was heavy with the scent of fresh pine sawdust, and their mother, weeks away from her death, held François's hand with her left and Pierre's in her right. Holding onto each other, they formed a ring and skipped in wide circles along to the lively music, their heads thrown back in laughter. They whirled, faster and faster, until everyone else in the barn was a blur, leaving only the three of them, happy in a world of their own.

The blacksmith looked down at his stew. It looked and smelled fantastic. He could see potatoes, corn and carrots interspersed with generous chunks of lamb. Rosalie quietly said, "Eat up," from her place by his elbow and she smiled at him, nervously it seemed. "It won't bite you."

He took a bite. It was fantastic. The gravy was thick, with just the right amount of spice, and the lamb flaked itself to bits at the pressure of his tongue against his teeth. He enjoyed another bite while Rosalie ate silently beside him. It wasn't until his third spoonful, when he bit into the carrot, that his world tipped sideways.

Then, like a nightmare come to life, he was there. Reinhabiting his body but not controlling it, at the curve of the river halfway between his forge and Rosalie's cottage. It was early spring and even earlier morning so the air was sharp enough to cut, as were his wife's words.

"You set the fire? You can't be serious," he heard himself stammer and felt the familiar knot, like an anvil, wedge itself in his stomach.

"I didn't mean to, it was an accident."

Her tears had no effect on the molten emotions sweeping through him. The grief he'd struggled with after Bella's death and the guilt he'd carried, certain his negligence had caused the fire, melted from him, making his limbs tremble. "I thought it was me. For weeks. I thought I'd killed her."

She looked at her feet for a moment but then met his gaze and shrugged. "I couldn't tell you, I was ashamed . . ."

All the anger and horror in his belly let go, like a spring attached to his arm. He felt his fist smash into her face. Her teeth scraped his knuckles and then her body fell backward and he heard the sound that haunted his dreams even now as her skull connected with a boulder, half-buried in the earth.

She didn't move. She wasn't breathing.

Tears coursed, unchecked, down his cheeks and each ragged breath he pulled into his lungs shook his body. "It was an accident," he whispered, and the words clouded the air before him. "I can't go to jail, the boys need me. It was an accident."

Still muttering to himself, he scooped her up and laid her in the river. The water washed the blood from her hair as he held her beneath the surface, but it didn't clean the accusations from her eyes.

Joseph choked on his dinner and tears coursed, like the creek, down his cheeks. Rosalie jumped to her feet, knocking her chair back and slapped him hard between his shoulder blades. Twice. Three times. Finally the food released its grip and he spat it into his hand and set it in his bowl where it remained, mangled and half-finished.

He'd relived the moments of his wife's death over and over in the months since it happened, but never so vividly, never so painfully as now. His mind whirled, like rapids, sweeping him away with it. The scent of the poppies, the carrots, the planted stories. "You're a witch," he snapped at Rosalie who watched him, fear and sadness in her eyes.

The boys stared silently from across the table, eyes wide and jaws stilled.

"We're going home," Joseph said, and the boys knew better than to argue with his tone. Offering sheepish smiles to their hostess they followed their father to the door. They had just stepped out of it when Rosalie called, "Enlightenment can be a good thing. Depending on what you do with it."

"Papa," François ventured once they were almost home. "What's wrong?"

"I choked is all," he answered gruffly. "And it scared me. Men do stupid things when they're scared."

"We can apologise when we see her again?" Pierre proposed tentatively.

"Yes. When we see her again."

Hours later, with the boys sleeping soundly in their beds, Joseph walked the road to Rosalie's cottage for the third time that night. His steps were slow but determined. He had no choice. She'd enlightened him all right. She knew. She knew, so she must be stopped. The boys needed their father.

As he drew near he could see her through a window. She was at her table, head bent over a piece of paper, writing furiously. He opened her door, filling its mouth with his bulk. She looked up at him and swallowed audibly. "You don't have to do this."

"I do." He answered. "I'm sorry, but I do. I can't risk keeping you around. You or your cursed vegetables."

She set her pen down and stepped slowly around the table, keeping it between the two of them. "You don't have to do this," she said again, her voice shaking. "Let me help you. You can explain—"

"How do you know?"

"I just . . . do. I get visions. I—you can explain. It was an accident—" tears spilled down her cheeks and clung to her eyelashes.

"I'm sorry," he said.

When it was done he ransacked the kitchen, gathered up all her vegetables and the remnants of the night's stew, carried it out to the outhouse and tossed it down the hole. When he bent to pick up her body, his eyes fell on the paper upon the table. He squinted at it. Its words were messier than usual and written around and over bell pepper seeds, and though he couldn't read what it said, he recognized his name.

He looked from the papers, their ink still wet, to the bound volumes on the fireplace. If he destroyed the books it would seem more likely Rosalie had gone of her own accord. Leaving them would be a giant arrow pointing to the fact something was wrong. He glanced at the fireplace, then shook his head. He couldn't risk burning them. If he did, he'd have to stay there and make sure they were completely destroyed, and he didn't have time to do that, dispense with Rosalie, and make it home before the boys woke.

Cursing, he gathered the books from the mantle, then grabbed the papers off the table and made one last trip to the outhouse. He fed the books, one by one, through the hole to join dinner, then tore up the pages from the table and let the pieces rain down from his fingertips into the darkness.

He carried Rosalie to the woods and left her for the wolves to find.

Her absence wasn't noticed for a couple weeks. She'd never been overly social, so when she missed a church service folk raised their eyebrows but didn't think much about it. It was only after the second time people became concerned enough to seek her out. They found the cottage empty, her beloved books missing. The weather had been exceptionally hot and without her hand to aid it, her garden had wilted, and everything that hadn't died had gone to seed. Shaking their heads at the peculiarity of some people, the villagers went back to report that she'd obviously gone off somewhere as precipitously as she'd appeared in the first place.

Summer crept into autumn, and Marie and Nicole took to using the lonely cottage to meet. It was at the conclusion of one such tryst, that after kissing Nicole goodbye, Marie returned to the cottage to pass time. The two girls made a point of never leaving or arriving at the village at the same time. It was best the whispers about them remain speculative.

When nature beckoned with urgent fingers, Marie slipped out into the evening and headed in the direction of the outhouse. The heat was like a wall, even now as the sun neared the horizon, but need was need and she pressed forward, only to find, much to her surprise, a veritable jungle of plants around the outhouse. They climbed up the walls, tumbled over one another and stretched curious tendrils out to crawl along the ground. Flowers and vegetables wrestled and danced here as they'd once done throughout the whole of Rosalie's garden. Marie had to work to open the door, but inside the outhouse was cool and dark, too dark for plants to grow and thus free of them. When she again emerged, however, she spent some time looking at the mangled foliage and tired blooms going to seed.

Her eye fell on an especially vibrant splash of green, and bending over she discovered a green pepper plant pressing itself up toward the sun, using the side of the privy for support. Three ripe peppers awaited harvest. She picked them, for surely Rosalie wouldn't begrudge her the vegetables in her absence. Joseph had been withdrawn lately, but green peppers were one of his favorites. They would be the perfect addition to the chili she planned to take to the church's potluck dinner this Sunday. Maybe, she thought as she made her way back toward town, vegetables in hand, that would help cheer him up.

# The Onion Prince

## *David Sklar*

### 1. Invitation

Have you ever tried peeling an onion from the inside out?
You start out perfect, small and round and sweet;
the onion's core surrounds you
and you eat the parts you've peeled away.

You work your way to wider spaces
where the skin gets drier,
but the eating makes you fatter
and you grow to fill the space you've made.

By night it's completely dark;
by day the light is diffuse and all around,
and the light gets ever brighter
with the peeling of each layer,
the light grows brighter every day on your red eyes.

### 2. Lament

"Great god who made the Onion, answer me:
My fingertips blister and under my cuticles bleed;
The skin of my genitals burns: I want an answer:
What will I know when I gnaw beyond this dome?
Is it softer there? Will the air not cook my eyes?
My fingers not need squeak on pungent walls?

Creator—Lord—I am more than what you made.
I know this burning vessel; know it well.
And now I ask. And now I need to know:
What is the World beyond the Onion's dome?"

### 3. Elegy

Amid baby oaks, in a vast expanse of sunlight
where only a little dappled shade got through
we laid out our picnic: blanket, basket, bread,
blender, frying pan, oven, table, chairs,

cracked an onion for our omelet—found a man
completely formed inside, in suit and tie
but limp like something pickled. Tiny man
whose life had ended, suffocated here.

We dug the smallest twig, less than a sapling,
a stem with just two leaves. We laid him there,
covered him over with earth, stripped the branch of bark,
left it on his grave, a monument, and wept.

# The Girl Who Learned to Live with Bees in Her Hair

*Brigitte N. McCray*

*1.*

When she came to the dead tree near the Roanoke River,
dark congregation of the hollowed out trunk
buzzing with invitation,
she did not mean to threaten the queen
with her honeyed lips,
the slender abdomen exposed
by her striped sports bra,
her own frenzied movement
brought on by the music humming
through iPod buds in her ears.
She couldn't detect the release of pheromone,
and when the swarm suddenly flew near,
the girl had no time to think
of how to transform into an attacking bird.
No need. The worker bees thought of her as their new queen
and settled in and around her thick red hair.

*2.*

At first, the girl ran faster and farther,
alongside the river, over the embankment,
the bees swarming behind her
as if she were a rich source of energy to forage.
Her legs cramped and her hips grew sore,
and so, when she came to a shallow water spot,
she halted. Her reflection:
the top of her head alive,
like a hundred mini-Christmas lights
electrifying her brain.

She sat then for hours on a river rock
as the bees built their honeycomb,
removing the fatty wax
from the folds of their skins,
their tiny feet kneading
her scalp as if they were concerned,
tension and anxiety knotty
under their mandibles,
and with the building up of cells, her body weighed sweet.

*3.*
She learned to deal with small annoyances:
teachers complaining about sticky essays and exams,
her dates getting stung as they tried to kiss her goodnight,
watery eyes and runny nose from the pollen-filled cells atop her head.

*4.*
In return, honey daily dripped down,
her tongue licking up before it reached her mouth,
the substance seeing her through the years.
In her forties, always carded,
she was easily mistaken for the girl she once was,
before her bees, in her early twenties.
Other women begged to lick a bit of the sweetness from her cheeks.
She would refuse, knowing that immortality's cruelty
is to live with endless shells of death:
the bees' life spans about five weeks,
she would sit rocking on her front porch,
waiting for the foragers, already beyond their prime,
to return to her hair.
She learned to sing ballads
that eased the flutter of their tired wings.
She spent days plucking the dead bees
from her windowsill, where they were dropped
by their fellow workers keeping their home clean.
She kept the bodies in a shoebox under her bed,
and, in the evening, before sleep, she would pull it out,
plunging her hands in deep, the crunch of carcasses
compelling her to whisper and whistle a soft, sad tune

as the bits of fur prickled her taut skin.
During the nights, honey slipping down her plastic-covered pillow,
when the buzzing quieted and the hundreds of feet softened their
    movement,
the woman dreamed of Tithonus, his babbling equal to her own tears.

# The Giant's Tree

## *Yukimi Ogawa*

His strides defined hills and plains. Where he jumped playfully, the footprints he left became lakes.

Haru looked down from his shoulder in awe; she always did. All her life she had been with the giant, and she still marveled at how whimsical he seemed, with the results so meticulous and beautiful. The ridges ran across the plain of red soil, and hills, woods and rivers ran from it like veins, reminding her of a leaf.

*Their* plain.

But now she saw her own legs dangling and sighed. They looked paler, fainter, as they always did before her departure. "Bo," she said to the giant, "I think I have to go soon."

"Really?" The giant's enormous head turned left to her; he looked at her and grunted. "I'll miss you. I wish at least you could tell how long it's going to take."

"Me, too. I'll bring as many memories as possible."

"Thanks, Haru."

Aki opened her eyes.

She slowly dragged herself out of the dream, which she didn't remember except for a lingering sense of something missing. Reluctantly she crawled out of her futon, which seemed so warm, the heat too complete, too enclosing to be of her own making. But now the warmth faded rapidly. She shook her pajamas off and changed.

Downstairs her breakfast was already waiting for her. She wrinkled her nose at the smell of natto, but smiled. "I think I want to give it a try this morning," she said to her mother.

"What? But you don't like natto."

"I had the dream."

"Oh."

The dream came to her every couple of years. She had first had the dream when she was three, and now she was ten and she'd had four or five of these dreams. She never remembered what the dream was about, but for a while after waking, everything looked brighter and clearer, as if an invisible filter had been removed from her eyes. She needed to *know*, to memorize, everything she could. The long-forgotten (to her) flavor of natto had to be recalled thoroughly, as if she had to teach someone else about it.

Now Aki chuckled at the sticky feel of the food. "Doesn't taste that bad, but I still don't like the smell."

"You don't have to finish it if you don't want to."

"I want to. Morning, Dad."

Her father came in, polishing his glasses. "You eating natto?"

"I had the dream."

Her father shook his head and sat down. Aki finished her breakfast quite happily, but brushed her teeth very carefully afterwards to scrub the flavor away.

AT SCHOOL AKI ran up to the sixth graders' floor, to the veranda overlooking the hills, rivers and forests. Then she went to the library and started devouring history books and maps. She opened the map of her district and pointed to the plain their town belonged to, and asked her friends if it didn't look like a leaf. None of them had ever thought of it that way, but now that she asked, perhaps it did, yes.

On her way home her best friend, Fumi, came running after Aki and caught up. "My mom's baking cakes today. Do you want to drop by?"

"Cakes can be baked at home?" Aki almost yelled. Her own mother wasn't a home-baking type.

Fumi laughed. "Of course. Come on."

As soon as Fumi slid the door to her house open, they could smell the sweet vanilla and chocolate scent wafting out. Aki inhaled deeply. "Oooooh, how nice."

As they waited for Fumi's mother to prepare their plates, Aki found a pamphlet about local legends, and the two girls read it aloud together. A few lines in the middle were dedicated to an ancient giant, who made a pyramid-shaped mountain over a lake in Haruna, a place to the west of their town. Aki trailed off in the middle of a sentence, and Fumi looked at her, surprised. "Aki, why are you crying?"

Aki touched her cheeks and found tears. "I don't know," she said, honestly. "I don't know."

Then Fumi's mother came in with a tray. "Here you go, girls! — Aki-chan? Are you all right?"

Aki smiled and took her plate. As she bit into her cupcake she chewed really slowly, trying to memorize the taste. Then she asked Fumi's mother about the ingredients. By the time she said goodbye to her friend, she had forgotten about crying.

HARU FOUND HERSELF lying curled on Bo's chest.

Bo himself was curled up in their cave like a small child, snoring ferociously and smiling, dreaming. Haru smiled and looked over at the mouth of the cave; the sky was still star-strewn and all was quiet. Bo's snore was so loud that no living thing slept or hunted around here at night. Haru was the only one who could put up with it. She'd been away a relatively short period. Last time Haru went away, it took her almost a month to come back.

She bit her lower lip to suppress the urge to shake him awake. With their difference in size, it was always a wonder to the girl how the giant would wake, no matter how subtle her shaking or patting, when Haru needed him.

But tonight Haru shook her thoughts away. Just as much as she wanted to talk to him, sleeping, surrounded by his presence, was a treat she had missed all week.

So she went back to sleep.

THE NEXT TIME she opened her eyes, she was afloat.

Haru looked around, rubbing at her eyes. Bo was sunk to his neck, only his bald head above the surface of the lake he had created for his bath. Haru was on a very crude boat Bo had made out of loose-knit grasses and leaves, which sooner or later would come apart.

Bo let out a laugh. "I was hoping to startle you when the thing broke and sank."

Haru wriggled and kicked, unraveling the raft. Then she swam to Bo's side and hugged his enormous arm. "This lake isn't even there in the times to come!" she said.

"What?" the giant said and sat up, filling the lake with huge waves.

Haru screamed an amused scream as the waves carried her off. Bo scooped her up and held her in front of his face. "They buried the lake," the little girl giggled. "They have these special tools to bury a lake, or flatten a mountain."

Bo shook his head and placed the girl on his shoulder. "Where would I bathe, then?"

"Sea, of course. It's so huge."

"But is it big enough for me?"

"Sure. And Bo, that mountain should be higher."

"But I've used up all the soil around it."

"You can use it from over there." Haru pointed, in the direction she had learned—*Aki* had learned—as south. "That land was lower, like a basin surrounded by hills. And . . . I think the river was wider." She squinted at the shining flow.

"That shouldn't be a problem. Rivers will get wider on their own in time."

"Will they?"

Bo nodded. "The land, we don't have to make it perfect. Those creatures sure know how to spoil what's been prepared for them, like what they'll do to my lake."

Haru chuckled, and looked up. Even the color of Aki's sky wasn't the same. Was it impossible to make a perfect world for humans?

"Oh, Bo. I need some seeds."

"What for?"

From his left shoulder, Haru reached out and touched his eyelid. Images washed through the giant—egg, wheat, sugarcane and other things. "Cake," she whispered. "It was so delicious—why can I only show you, but never let you *taste* it?"

Bo grinned. "Mmm. Okay, let's get the seeds then."

The two looked up into the sky. Haru watched as Bo willed the sky to change so it looked like night, only it was a little lighter. It reminded Haru of sunshine twinkling through a green canopy thick with leaves.

The giant reached out. And at that moment his arm became very long—or the sky drew close to them, Haru didn't know which was the case—and his hand closed around a cluster of stars. When his arm came back his hand was full of seeds.

"Today, let's prepare dry lands for the powder thing, and humid fields for the sweet thing . . . Will be a busy day." Bo grinned again, baring his teeth like tombstones.

Haru nodded and hugged the giant's head.

AKI WAS LOOKING up at the ancient, huge zelkova tree on the school grounds when Fumi found her. Their graduation ceremony had just ended, and other sixth graders were scattered around the ground, taking photos or exchanging messages on the blank pages of their yearbooks. Fumi trotted up until she stood beside Aki. "You always liked this tree, didn't you?" she asked.

"Not always," Aki said. "Since last year, when I had another dream. For some reason it keeps reminding me of someone I don't remember. Funny?"

Fumi shook her head. "Your dreams have always been so mysterious. Remember the field trip to the mountain a few years back? You helped our team a lot in the trekking competition, telling us which way to go find the landmarks, though you'd never been there."

"Perhaps I had. When I was really small or something. Perhaps I just don't remember."

"Perhaps. But when you look at this tree, you look as if you are in love with it."

Aki blushed, even knowing it was nonsense. "I'll miss this tree," she muttered after a while.

Fumi nodded and smiled. "We can always come back here, you know. It's not going anywhere."

Aki nodded back, and said nothing.

HARU CIRCLED AROUND the baby zelkova tree. This one was the first of the race, grown from one of Bo's seeds, and so grew very slowly, so that it would live long and produce many seeds of its own in the times to come. Bo let her bury the seed and nurture it; it was the first time Bo entrusted her with any life. He'd said she was big enough now to handle it.

Bo found her patting lovingly at the bark. He chuckled. "You really love that tree, don't you?"

Haru turned to look at him. "You don't understand. It's still there in thousands of years. Feels just like we ourselves are still there."

"I wish I could see it for myself, too, with you."

"Why am I the only one going to see the times to come?"

Bo only shook his head.

Later that night, she felt a chilly wind swirling around her and woke up. Bo seemed undisturbed and snored on. Haru stood and walked out of the cave, down the slope to the riverside. The moon shone on the river, the reflection quavered a little unnaturally and a creature, of Haru's own race, appeared out of the water. It found Haru and smiled. It was male, like Bo.

He came to stand in front of Haru. "The earth shaped me to be your partner," he said, smiling shyly.

Haru blinked, in surprise and confusion. "But . . . but I have Bo."

"He is not made for you."

Of course, she had thought about it. Other creatures around them, foxes, butterflies and sparrows and everything, all matched so perfectly, while Bo and Haru were so different. Haru had started vaguely wondering if she would ever grow to be Bo's size. But . . .

The he-creature tilted his head. "We are going to be the first, real couple of our race."

"Then what about Bo?"

He shook his head. "Sorry. He cannot survive in the times to come. His role is ending."

"But . . ." Tears suddenly welled out of Haru's eyes. "But . . ."

He stepped closer to her, touched her cheek and for some reason Haru couldn't imagine, pressed his lips to hers. "I'm sorry," he said. Haru tasted salt and river and moon. "I'm sorry, I didn't mean to hurt you." He pressed his lips again.

Then Haru, surprised at her own reaction, kissed him back.

Lost in this new experience, she didn't realize, until a long time later, that Bo's snoring had stopped.

When he knew Haru was lost to him, Bo collapsed, and countless seeds, just too many of them for even Haru to comprehend, exploded into the world. His flesh nurtured the plain. On this plain, humans, Haru's children, thrived. Only the remnants of Bo's snore got trapped in the mountain cave, and remained there and shook the earth from time to time.

And Aki stopped having the dreams.

For a few years Aki missed the strange feelings brought by the dreams. When these feelings began to fade, and the *missing* began to fade, she wanted badly to fill the hollow. The first time a man tried to court her, with no thought at all she leapt into his arms.

The feel of his arms was *different,* wrong. But she ignored the difference, because she had no idea what it was different from. She followed the man to a town facing the sea, and dreamed of her children bathing in the water.

AND NOW, AKI stood at the foot of the huge zelkova tree in her hometown.

It had taken three years to find out that her husband was infertile. Aki said to him she was okay, she didn't care. But in truth it was not okay at all, she really cared, and her husband seemed to sense that. He started doubting her love, which was in fact starting to fade, and so he started ignoring her.

So Aki came back to her town, where there was no sea or lake. She was still in touch with Fumi, but Fumi had left the town long ago. Aki wondered about the buzz in her chest, attributed it to the loneliness, the aftermath of putting an end to a relationship and having no friend to talk to about it. When one Sunday she realized it wasn't just these things, she went out of her parent's house and sneaked into her old elementary school to gaze up at the tree.

She missed the dreams, in which she knew she had a place, safe and comfortable, to go back to; now she couldn't remember where it was. Or if such a place had ever existed. She started to cry, saw the tree blur with tears, when she heard footsteps approaching.

They stopped a little behind her. "Ma'am." A man's voice. "Unauthorized entry is strictly prohibited here. May I see your ID?"

Aki flinched and turned around, eyes still a little watery. "I'm sorry. I'm a graduate here and wanted to see the tree—"

And it was the man's turn to flinch, as he saw her eyes full of tears. "Sorry. Sorry, I was just kidding. I'm no authority here. I myself sneaked in because I saw the tree from the road and—"

Aki watched him as he said three or four more sorries. He was a tall man, his head shaved, sturdily built and somewhat intimidating. But his eyes looked warm to her—silly, of course; she didn't know this man, warm or cold.

When Aki said nothing in reply for a while, the man blushed and said, "Do you know how old this tree is?"

Aki shook her head, smile invading her face despite herself. "No, *sir*. No one knows for sure."

The man grew even redder. "Oh, please. I'm sorry."

She burst out laughing, wiped her tears and went to stand beside the man. "You're not from around here?"

"No," he shook his head. "My ancestors lived here, and we have the family tomb not far from here. I just went there and saw this tree on the way back. Such a huge tree—so you played and studied under it?"

"Yes, it was one of us, really. Our friend. Pupils all loved it."

The man looked somehow happy to hear it, and they both looked up, side by side. Then he let out a deep, warm laugh. "The foliage is so dense," he said and reached out his arm towards the canopy, as if he thought he could touch the leaves if he tried. "I know this must sound silly, but it reminds me of something . . . something I used to be able to reach . . . I don't know, can't explain well enough . . ."

The man trailed off, because he caught Aki looking at him.

The tears had come back into her eyes. The moment she had heard him laugh she knew, just knew what she *had* to say. When the man stretched his arm upwards there was no doubt about it. When their eyes met, she only followed the sentence that was ringing in her head. "How would you like some cakes?"

He blinked in surprise. But soon—too soon—grinned. "I'd like that very much."

Tears found their way down her cheeks, but Aki smiled. He never questioned her tears, or the sudden change of subject. She invited him to her house, where she would bake cupcakes for them both. Vanilla and chocolate. And in the years to come, they would start building their own realm, which was called home.

# Two Ways of Lifting

## *Virginia M. Mohlere*

*For Amal El-Mohtar*

The bar feels at home in her hands,
    after years of sweat,
        lactic acid,
        the stupid constant search for "enough protein"
        (when all she wants is an apple).

The dead
lift
brought her shoulders to life,
sculpted a marble-worthy back.
The lift
deadened her
    (she hopes, but knows better)
to covert dudely stares
skeptical (read: upset)
to be out-
lifted
by "a girl."
        The gym of her perfect heaven
        might have as many as *two* other women in it.

On a December morning,
she does not think of metal
when she hears about the doe.
But when her eye hits binocular,
her hands itch.
The urge for weight

deadens
her worry,
lifts
her outside to the animal terrified on ice.

Her back is certain,
legs eager.
Her hands will not be guided
by her surprise-sparking brain.

She grasps; braces.
The live lift
is not so graceful,
    but her arms are full of deer,
    carried past danger.
She makes a tick on her workout log
in a whole new category.

# Levels of Observation

## *Kenneth Schneyer*

*From the Primary Level Placement and Tracking Assessment, administered at age 7:*

10. Look at the four pictures below. Which one is the sad face?

    a. Face A.
    b. Face B.
    c. Face C.
    d. Face D.

11. After you walked in the front door of this building, how many times did you turn a corner before you got to this room?

    a. 5.
    b. 7.
    c. 9.
    d. 11.

12. Which of these things was in your father's or mother's pockets when they walked with you in the hallway this morning? You can pick more than one.

    a. Nothing.
    b. A wallet.
    c. A knife or gun.
    d. Something else.
    e. I don't know.

13. Press the blue button. When the blue light comes on, answer: Do you think anyone is looking at you right now?

a. Yes, one person is looking at me.
b. Yes, three people are looking at me.
c. No one is looking at me.
d. I can't tell.

14. Press the red button, and an exam helper will come to your seat. After the exam helper arrives, answer this question: Does the exam helper like to eat:

a. Pizza?
b. Hot dogs?
c. Noodles?
d. Tacos?

15. Press the green button and a window will open. You will see four women sitting in chairs, with numbers on their backs. Which one is keeping a secret?

a. Number 1.
b. Number 2.
c. Number 3.
d. Number 4.

16. Is it a nice secret or a nasty secret?

a. A nice secret.
b. A nasty secret.

*From the Developmental Adjustment & Orientation Inventory, administered to Eighth-Year Students:*

28. My talent is:

a. A blessing.
b. A useful tool in the service of a good cause.
c. An irritating habit that sometimes comes in handy.
d. A curse.

29. It's right for me to know:

    a. Anything I can find out.
    b. Anything that helps me serve others and improve the world.
    c. Anything that doesn't hurt anybody else.
    d. Only what people want me to know about them.

30. My teachers:

    a. Are cruel.
    b. Don't care about me one way or the other.
    c. Are willing to hurt me if it will help them accomplish important goals.
    d. Want what is best for me.
    e. Love me.

31. My parents:

    a. Are the best people to advise me in all things.
    b. Love me, but do not understand the needs and goals of someone with talents like mine.
    c. Have no idea what my life is like.

32. I can trust (circle all that apply):

    a. My teachers.
    b. My fellow students.
    c. My family.
    d. No one.

*From the Academy Comprehensive Certification Examination:*

72. When is authorization by a Desk Officer required before commencing Level Two Observation of a subject?

    a. In all cases except where there is an imminent threat to human life or public safety.

b. In all cases except where the Observer has probable cause to believe that evidence of a crime will be disclosed.
c. It is never required.

73. When is authorization by a Desk Officer required before commencing Level Three Observation of a subject?

a. In all cases.
b. In all cases except where there is an imminent threat to human life or public safety.
c. In all cases except where there is an imminent danger of mission failure.

74. During Level Two Observation, a subject's feelings and emotional state are:

a. Dangerous.
b. Distractions that should be ignored.
c. Harmless noise.
d. Data that should be recorded.
e. Useful tools for influencing the subject in the future.

75. How long can continuous Level Two Observation be maintained without risk of personality disorientation to the Observer?

a. 5 hours.
b. 10 hours.
c. 15 hours.
d. 20 hours.

76. How long can continuous Level Three Observation be maintained without risk of personality disorientation to the Observer?

a. 30 minutes.
b. 60 minutes.
c. 90 minutes.
d. There is no period without such risk.

77. Practicum Problem A: When you are ready, notify the proctor.

The proctor will lead you to an interrogation room containing one subject, one certified Observer, and three other candidates. When the proctor gives the signal, commence Level Two Observation of the subject *only*, assessing all mandatory and desirable objects. After 30 minutes, write a report of your Observations and give them to the proctor. Candidate reports will be compared to the report of the certified Observer. *Any candidate practicing Level Three Observation during this examination will be dismissed.*

*From Form 29-J-7, Post-Observation Log, Variation 7:*

5. Duration of Observation:

6. Location of Subject when Observation commenced:

7. Location of Subject when Observation terminated:

8. Level of Observation (check one): II III

For the remaining questions (except for question 17), you will be permitted only 20 seconds for each answer.

9. Describe the meal you ate most recently before commencing Observation.

10. Name the last person with whom you had a conversation before commencing Observation:

11. Are you (check as many as apply):

    angry frightened sad jealous irritated
    annoyed frustrated confused euphoric

12. What is your political affiliation?

13. Do you believe in a god?

14. Do you prefer wine, beer, or spirits?

15. Whom do you love?

16. Whom do you hate?

17. List at least five ways in which you are *different from* the subject of the Observation:

*From the Nomination Questionnaire for the Outstanding Service Medal:*

7. What was the duration of the longest Level Two Observation completed by the nominee?

   a. Less than 24 hours.
   b. 24–48 hours.
   c. More than 48 hours.

8. What was the duration of the longest Level Three Observation completed by the nominee?

   a. Less than 1 hour.
   b. 1–2 hours.
   c. More than 2 hours.

9. Using percentages, indicate the approximate breakdown of characteristics of the nominee's Level Two and Level Three subjects. (In case of overlap, it is acceptable to exceed 100%.)

   a. Unwilling witnesses:
   b. Crime victims:
   c. Members of criminal/terrorist organizations:
   d. Enemy agents:
   e. Persons suspected of conspiracy to commit:
      i. Violent crime:
      ii. Property crime:
      iii. Treason:

10. Of the nominee's Level Two Observations, approximately how many resulted in:

    a. Production of usable material evidence?
    b. Identification of new subjects?
    c. Positive identification of criminals?
    d. Arrests?
    e. Incarcerations?

11. Of the nominee's Level Three Observations, how many resulted in:

    a. Prevention without surrender to police?
    b. Surrender to police without confession?
    c. Confession?
    d. Suicide?

*From the Level Three Observation Ancillary Effects Report:*

5. How many persons other than the intended subject were affected by Level Three Observation?

6. Indicate how far each of these persons was from the intended subject at the time of Level Three Observation.

    a. Number within 10 feet of subject:
    b. Number between 11 and 20 feet from subject:
    c. Number beyond 20 feet from subject:

*(If the number in #6(c) is greater than zero, refer to Training Division.)*

7. Were any of the affected persons minor children? If so, how many?

8. Are any of the affected persons now deceased? If so, how many?

*(If the response to #8 is in the affirmative, refer to Compensation Department.)*

*From the Observer Oversight Log:*

22. Has the Observer expressed reluctance to engage in Level Two or Level Three Observation? If so, provide details.

23. Has the Observer expressed sympathy with criminal subjects? If so, provide details.

24. Has the Observer expressed disagreement with the aims or methods of the Division? If so, provide details.

25. Has the Observer displayed any confusion concerning his/her own motives, beliefs, or identity? If so, provide details and refer to Division Counseling.

*From the Division Counseling and Referral Intake:*

6. When did you first experience the problem for which you are visiting today?

7. Why do you think this problem is related to one of your Observation sessions?

8. Do you think you are in danger of:

    a. Hurting yourself?
    b. Committing violence against others?
    c. Jeopardizing the mission of the Division?

9. Have you actually attempted to do any of the above? If so, specify.

10. Have you refused any assignments or disobeyed any orders during the last 72 hours?

11. If possible, identify the subject of the last Observation session that preceded the problems you have noticed.

*From the Level Three Observation Failure Report:*

7. Outcome of Observation:

a. Anticipated crime was committed (specify).
b. Subject did not confess.
c. Subject did not turn him/herself in for arrest.
d. Subject did not commit suicide.
e. Subject committed suicide when not authorized.

8. Current status of subject (check as many as apply):

a. No change in previous status.
b. Changed location (specify).
c. New crime probability (specify).
d. Alerted to Level Three Observations.
e. Deceased.

9. Probable reason for failure:

a. Insufficient Observer range/duration (*refer to Desk Officer*).
b. Subject with undocumented Observation abilities (*refer to Special Investigations*).
c. Misidentification of subject (*refer to Quality Control*).
d. Observer error (*refer to Training Division*).
e. Observer noncompliance (*refer to Internal Affairs*).

*From the Internal Affairs Referral Cover Sheet:*

4. What is the probable/suspected reason for the Observer noncompliance? (Check as many as apply.)

a. Personality disorientation or emotional fusion.
b. Fatigue.
c. Other mental disorder (specify).
d. Corruption / criminal activities (specify).
e. Political resistance / treason.

5. Current status of Observer:

   a. Desk duty.
   b. Temporary leave.
   c. In custody.
   d. Under medical observation.
   e. Whereabouts unknown.

*From the Observer Detention Intake Inventory:*

17. Prisoner's certified Level Two Observation range (when in doubt, *over*estimate):

    a. Less than 100 feet.
    b. 100–299 feet.
    c. 300–499 feet.
    d. 500 feet or more.

18. Prisoner's certified Level Three Observation range (when in doubt, *over*estimate):

    a. Less than 20 feet.
    b. 20–49 feet.
    c. 50–69 feet.
    d. 70–89 feet.
    e. 90 feet or more.

19. Has an assessment been performed of the prisoner's probable long-term response to isolation? If so, summarize it:

20. How susceptible is the prisoner to Level Two Observation?
    a. Fully transparent. (Attach explanation.)
    b. Partially transparent.
    c. Primarily opaque with exceptions.
    d. Fully opaque (i.e., standard Observer profile).

21. How susceptible is the prisoner to Level Three Observation?

a. Fully compliant.
b. Mostly compliant, with exceptions.
c. Mostly resistant, with exceptions (i.e., standard Observer profile).
d. Impervious.

22. The period of the mandated detention:

a. Less than 180 days.
b. 180 days–2 years.
c. 2–5 years.
d. More than 5 years.
e. Life.

*From the Level Four Observation Authorization and Mandate:*

31. Documented Level Three Observation range of subject (update if possible):

32. Names of at least five (5) certified Observers to commence Level Four Observation, with the certified Level Three range of each. (*Authorization will be denied unless* all *ranges listed are greater than the range specified in #31*):

33. For each Observer listed in #32, attach signed orders for temporary leave of at least 60 days commencing immediately after completion of Level Four Observation. (*Authorization will be denied unless* all *orders are attached.*)

34. Psychiatric assessor authorizing Level Four Observation:

35. District director authorizing Level Four Observation:

36. Regional commander authorizing Level Four Observation:

37. Facility warden authorizing Level Four Observation:

38. Contact information for subject's next of kin:

*Copies of this Authorization and Mandate must be provided to the District director, regional commander, psychiatric assessor, facility warden, clerk's office, all Observers participating in the Level Four Observation and their Desk Officers. If next of kin is unavailable, consult District protocols for disposition of remains.*

# Cat's Canticle

## *David Sklar*

If you speak I will not answer,
if you call I will not come,
if you throw things at my shadow
I will nail them to your thumb.

You can call me by a name
that you are quite convinced is mine,
but the name by which you call me
I left out for you to find;

the name that guides my hand I carry
locked inside a box,
in an egg, inside a sparrow,
in the belly of a fox.

If you speak I will not answer,
if you call I will not come,
if you throw things at my shadow
I will nail them to your thumb,

but when you call the name that I have
crafted out of clay,
I'll catch your breath inside a bottle,
sealed with wax to make it stay.

# Nisei

*Beth Cato*

grandpa used to say
he joined the army to be like
all the other boys

he signed up from Manzanar
"I was as American as them"

he served in Japan after the bombs dropped
he brought the kappa back to California
said he found its pond nearly dried up
the house nearby a shattered ruin

he made the kappa a new garden
gravel rocks raked in sinuous swirls
cherry maple leaves like blood
upon the velvet carpet of moss
pond warmed by the Valencia sun

I would visit and bring cucumbers
to plunk on lily pad-capped water
the kappa grabbed the vegetables
with his long, webbed fingers
his skin green and slick like a frog
a fringed pate crowned his head and held
the water that kept him alive

they played jokes on each other
grandpa and the water imp
a string of trip wire across the path
grandpa's favorite chair, water-soaked
a gentle friendship of fifty years

but the kappa never touched the American flag
there in the center of the garden

sometimes the two of them sat there in evenings
tea cup nestled on the swell of grandpa's belly
kappa crouched at water's edge
red, white, and blue rippling in pink twilight
saying nothing, everything

# Echoes in the Dark

## *Ken Liu*

*A True and Correct Account of the Adventures of Captain John James Carrington in the Chinese Empire*

To welcome me to Shanghai, the American Consul General hosted a banquet in my honor.

The Chinese waiters streamed to and fro, bringing an endless array of foods exotic and strange to me: roasted duck dipped in rice wine, chilled longan fruit shaped like eyes, shrimp carved to resemble lutes. They worked efficiently and quietly, their Oriental faces impassive and inscrutable.

As we dined, I sought information on the leader of the rebels, a man nicknamed the Soaring Bat.

"The Chinese speak of him as a great fighter," my cousin said, "skilled in the ancient arts of combat. They call him by the honorific *Ta Tsia*, which I'm told means 'Great Hero.' Many are the tales of his prowess in battle and generosity towards the poor and helpless."

My cousin, a water engineer with the International Settlement, had invited me to Shanghai to advise them on security preparations. There was talk of a plot afoot by a group of Chinese fanatics, remnants of the Taiping Rebellion, to poison the water supply of the various treaty ports to discourage the expansion of foreign enclaves in China, which the rebels viewed as an outrage. The American residents of Shanghai did not trust that the incompetent and craven mandarins of the Ch'ing Court would properly protect the International Settlement.

"Oh, he is but a mirage," said another man, the owner of a steamship line. "The Chinese exaggerate this phantasm to assuage their foolish pride. Even if he exists, he is surely like his countrymen, a feeble opium addict who will crumple at the first demonstration of Western arms."

"Shanghai is a small haven in a populous and vast land," I said. "It behooves us to be respectful of our opponents."

I was used to men like him, men who thought fighting a game. But I had seen too much bloodshed at Shiloh and Gettysburg. After the conclusion of the Great Rebellion in 1865, I had sought to lay down the sword for the plow and find solace in my apple orchard outside Providence, Rhode Island. But here I was, a few years later, my revolver and sword by my side, far from home. In the eyes of the world, sometimes a soldier is always a soldier.

The man laughed. "The Chinese are a declining race, destined to fade from the stage of history. Have you forgotten that Commander Frederick Townsend Ward was able to defeat the Taiping hordes and protect Shanghai with only a ragtag team of a hundred deserters, discharged seamen, and drifters? Treat your time here as a holiday, Captain, for there is no threat."

I resolved to learn more about the facts before forming an opinion.

DURING THE NEXT few days, I traveled around Shanghai to study her defenses and evaluate the security of her water supplies.

The city lived up to her tawdry reputation. Every street corner seemed to hold a storytelling pavilion, where singsong girls performed their *t'antz'u* to slovenly and lascivious crowds. Servile and sickly men emerged from the opium dens behind bamboo fences.

But what made the greatest impression on me was a walk down Fourth Avenue at sunset, as the streets were filled with young Chinese women full of the most bold coquetry and seductive gestures, so that I thought even the most stalwart man would have been tempted.

I wondered if the man at my welcome banquet had been right about this decadent and indolent land.

ABOUT A WEEK after my arrival, I went on a survey of the rural countryside around Shanghai to scout for possible alternate sources of water that could be secured in the event of a rebel assault.

While on a stretch of road between two villages, my wagon suddenly stopped because a herd of pigs blocked the road. As my porters went up to shoo them away, masked men jumped out of the tall grass by the side of the road and surrounded us.

The cowardly porters immediately abandoned me and ran away. I managed to get off two shots with my revolver and might have wounded one of the bandits, but the others overwhelmed me and made me their prisoner.

The bandits blindfolded me and brought me on a long trek uphill.

Eventually, I was tied to a chair and my blindfold removed. But it might as well have been kept on, for I found myself in almost complete darkness.

"I'm sorry for the way you were invited here." A voice spoke out of the darkness. The man's accent was heavy, but he spoke slowly and softly and I easily understood him. "Some of my men are servants at the American Consulate. They speak highly of you as a man with an open mind."

Though startled, I strove to remain calm. "Who are you?"

"My name is Ts'ai Ch'iang-Kuo, the last of the Taiping commanders. I was born sightless, and I've learned that it is better to try to converse with the sighted in darkness. It seems to make you more willing to listen. The Ch'ing generals call me the Soaring Bat to mock me, but I've grown to like it."

Now that I had some time to orient myself in the darkness, I saw that I was in a small room, barely ten feet from wall to wall. A bit of light from a lamp in the next room leaked in under the door, and I could hear the sounds of men shuffling playing cards on the other side.

I could just make out by the faint light the figure of a tall man sitting on the bed across from my chair, his legs crossed under him. His hair, I saw, was long and worn loose, not in a queue, and his forehead was not shaven as was the custom in China. I vaguely recalled hearing that this meant he refused to submit to the Manchu Emperor.

"Whatever you're planning," I said, "it will not work. Shanghai is well armed and whether you like it or not, we own Shanghai and we're not leaving."

My interlocutor sighed. "Captain Carrington, we have no quarrel with you or your people. The rumors you hear of my ill intentions are spread by the Ch'ing mandarins."

"What?"

"You must know that the Heavenly Kingdom of Taiping is a Christian rebellion. I myself studied with an American missionary as a child and learned much to admire about your people."

I had heard that that the Taiping did purport to be a strange sect of Christians. "Yet your commanders threatened to run all foreigners into the sea."

"I cannot speak for all the Taiping forces. But our goal was to overthrow the Ch'ing. China is a country under occupation, Captain. The Manchu Emperor and his noblemen believe that this land is their private garden, and the people of China are their slaves. Think, Captain, what kind of ruler would rather slaughter his subjects than defend their lives against foreign gunboats? Until we put an end to this dynasty, the Chinese will not have justice or freedom."

His goals were ones I could sympathize with, if true. "Why have you kidnapped me then?"

"The Ch'ing Court manipulates France, Britain, and the United States to help solidify its rule against China's people. Perhaps your governments prefer to support it in exchange for favors and profitable concessions. But that is shortsighted. I brought you here to ask a favor of you."

But before my captor could say more, a lone, loud whistle rang out in the silence of the night, like a bird soaring into the sky, followed by a loud explosion.

"Signal rockets," my captor said. "The Ch'ing forces have surrounded us. They're eager to prevent you from hearing what I have to say. No matter. Come with me."

THE FORTRESS WAS built within the ruins of an old Buddhist temple carved into a cave at the foot of steep cliffs. In front of the cave was a large walled courtyard roughly square in shape.

Ts'ai and I crouched within a small chamber at the southwestern corner of the courtyard. Through a crack in the walls I was able to see the scene outside.

Torchlight revealed about a hundred Ch'ing soldiers with muskets and spears approaching the courtyard, the flickering light glinting from their weapons.

To mount an assault on the temple, the attackers must first scale the walls of the courtyard and cross the empty space. Logically, I would have expected the rebels to defend themselves by manning the walls.

But the walls were empty.

Ts'ai leaned over and whispered in my ear, "This is an old trick I learned from the peerless Chuge Liang, Prime Advisor to the Han centuries ago. The appearance of an undefended city will lead them to suspect a planned ambush. With their torches, they'll be easy targets. So they'll choose to fight blind, like me."

Indeed, within moments, I could hear the Ch'ing commander giving urgent orders in hushed tones, and the torches were quickly extinguished. It was a night of the new moon and overcast. All was now inky darkness.

I nodded, impressed with my host's tactical acumen. Without firing a single shot, he had induced a measure of anxiety into the enemy and caused them to voluntarily give up one of their advantages. He might not have gone to West Point, but he would have done well as a Union commander during the Great Rebellion.

But I still didn't understand his plan for victory. During our rush to hide in this chamber, I noted only about two dozen rebels inside the compound, and no muskets. It also stood to reason that the government forces would be better-equipped and disciplined. Even in complete darkness, it still seemed that the odds were against Ts'ai.

Indeed, I could hear ladders being propped against walls, and the muffled sounds of men climbing up and jumping down. A few minutes later, I guessed that the bulk of the Ch'ing forces were now inside the courtyard. Although there must have been more than eighty men in the courtyard, they were extraordinarily quiet, and there was no way to tell where exactly they were.

Then Ts'ai did something that I shall never forget. He began to hum.

It was halfway between a song and a moan, deeply resonant. Sometimes he seemed to be saying "om" and other times he seemed to be saying "nam." I could feel the sound vibrating in the walls around me, and I could hear it echoing in the silent night air.

He would hum for a few seconds, stop, and cock his ear to intently listen. Then he would change the pattern of his humming, altering pitch, duration, rhythm. It sounded like the description a New Bedford whaleman once gave me of the singing of the great fish.

I began to hear other sounds as well, the sound of men screaming in death. At first the sounds came singly, seriatim. But soon the screams merged into each other, rose to a crescendo, and I could feel the fear, the panic, the despair in the pleadings for mercy against unseen enemies in the night.

The fading sound of a horse's hoofs told me that the Ch'ing commander had abandoned his men and left. The screams of the dying gradually quieted, and all was again darkness and silence.

I let out an explosive breath that I had not realized I was holding. I was just about to speak to Ts'ai when the wooden door to the stone chamber flew open and a Ch'ing soldier stumbled inside, brandishing his spear.

A few arrows stuck out his back, and blood flowed freely from his wounds. As he careened around the room, I pressed myself against the wall and felt hot drops of blood splattering onto me. His movements were powerful but chaotic, the last throes of a dying man.

My host was completely still and quiet. Crouching in the dark, he was no doubt hoping to strike a fatal blow against the wounded soldier without being impaled on his frenzied spear first.

Now, this was my chance to turn the tables on my captor. I could assist the Ch'ing soldier, subdue the Soaring Bat, and claim a reward from the Chinese government as well as the gratitude of the International Settlement.

But I remembered Ts'ai's words, and I realized that I liked him. A soldier knows when to trust his instincts.

I lunged forward and twisted the spear out of the soldier's grasp. Using it like a bayonet, I ended his life with one quick thrust.

"Thank you," Ts'ai said.

IN THE LIGHT of the morning, as Ts'ai enjoyed the warm sunlight on a stone stool and sipped his tea, I carefully examined the courtyard and tried to reconstruct what had happened.

Here, I have with me a rough sketch I drew of the place. It is the same sketch that I later used in my application for a letter patent filed after I returned to America.

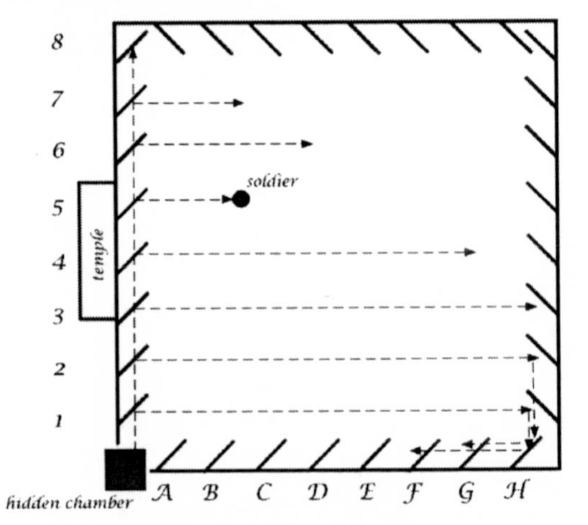

The angled baffles against the walls were made of hard and smooth slabs of stone. As I clapped my hands before it I could hear the crisp way the sound rebounded from it.

"These were constructed using the same material as the famed Echo Wall at the Temple of Heaven in Peking," Ts'ai said. "Sound does not die against it, but rather bounces off cleanly."

I gently touched the walls, cold and polished, not understanding.

Smiling with his sunken eyelids shut, my host continued. "Blindness gives me an advantage. My school of martial art has had many blind masters in its past. They refined the art of night fighting, where one uses ears to substitute for eyes. These stones and their use were passed down to me from these ancient masters."

When Ts'ai was humming last night, he had directed his sound to travel along the western wall, such that the sound would be deflected by each of the baffles along the indicated path in my diagram. A single sound was thus split into eight echoes, each of which crossed the courtyard along a latitudinal line. At the eastern wall the echoes were deflected again into a southerly direction until the baffles along the southern wall sent them back towards Ts'ai in the corner room.

Since each of the echoes traveled a different distance before arriving back at the chamber in which we hid, they accumulated together in Ts'ai's ear as a long, gradually diminishing echo.

"It sounds like the string on a *kuch'in* slowly returning to rest."

However, when something was in the courtyard (for example, a Ch'ing soldier), one of the eight echoes would be absorbed at the obstruction's location, resulting in a slight dip in the expected sound. If I map out the amplitude of sound over time, it would look something like this:

"You can tell when the dip in sound occurs?"

Ts'ai smiled proudly. He stood tall, the sun on his face, his back as straight as a pine tree. "It's a simple trick. All that is required is practice, concentration, and the ability to focus *chi*."

Similarly, Ts'ai's humming also was deflected at the northwestern corner to travel along the northern wall, where it was again deflected into eight separate echoes traversing the courtyard from north to south. If an obstacle in the courtyard intercepted one of these echoes, there would also be a slight dip in the expected sound.

Together, the eight echoes going east-west and the eight echoes going north-south divided the courtyard into a grid of sixty-four squares. Based on when the dips in the returning long echo occurred, Ts'ai could use his ears to "see" where enemy soldiers were. For instance, in my drawings, he would see that a soldier was standing at the square marked by the coordinates *B* and *5*.

If other soldiers stood elsewhere in the courtyard, there would be more dips in the echoes he heard. But of course Ts'ai did not use coordinates like mine.

"The sixty-four positions are named after the sixty-four hexagrams of the *I Ching*. My followers and I use a code so that by altering the patterns in my humming, I can call out each of the squares. Last night, my men hid inside the temple and concentrated their arrows in the darkness at where I told them the Ch'ing troops were. They shot without having to aim, using me as their eyes. And that was how we won."

TS'AI'S FAVOR TURNED out to be a request for me to act as an emissary to the International Settlement, and to the governments of Britain, France, and the United States.

"Soldier to solider, I ask you to persuade them to stop supporting the Ch'ing. Surely you see they're unworthy of the support of Christian nations."

I explained to him that in my experience, governments, even Christian ones, tended to favor winners. After all, Britain was willing to support the slave states of the Confederacy until she saw that the Union's victory was inevitable. If he wished for Western nations to stop propping up the Manchus, then the Chinese would have to show that they were capable of winning freedom on their own. It was a harsh lesson, but in my view, necessary.

He cocked his head, and smiled. "You believe that we must claim what we want by our own strength of arms."

"Yes."

"Even if that means someday we may ask your people to leave Shanghai and return it to us."

I considered this, and reluctantly agreed. "Such is the way of the world."

"Thank you," he said. "You're indeed a man of honor."

"I should be thanking you."

He asked what I meant.

I shared with him my excitement at learning the secret of his method of sightless detection. I could already see how this technique of seeing by sounds and echoes could be improved by science and apply to numerous arts in both war and peace.

Bringing to bear the principles of the phonautograph, which I had heard described by an acquaintance who had visited Édouard-Léon Scott in France, I thought it possible to transform the echoes into visible traces on paper, thus allowing an untrained man to match the skill of a master martial artist's ears. As well, using the motive force of electricity and ingenious mechanical clockwork, I could imagine *automatic* actions to be triggered upon the detection of an object.

My mind raced with possibilities. I had seen the first underwater warships deployed during the War for which no practical means of detection existed. But with this system of sound pulses installed near a harbor or shipping lanes, subsurface boats could be "seen" without sight. Also, banks and vaults would pay dearly for a system that could detect the presence of intruders and would-be robbers in complete darkness. And these were just scratching the surface.

As I described these visions to Ts'ai, his face went through a series of emotions: amusement, wonder, fear, then resignation.

"What is the matter? Master Ts'ai?"

"I am struck by the difference between our civilizations. My teachers and I have studied and passed on this ancient technique for generations as a means to compensate for a personal weakness. But you saw something I never could: an invention that would be useful to many more by the addition of mechanical engines to magnify human forces and senses."

"This is the age of invention," I said. "All nations' fates depend on it."

He became silent and thoughtful. At length he said, "My ancestors were once a people full of invention, too." He paused, and then added, "Perhaps we will be again, someday."

Together, in silence, we contemplated the fickle fortunes of nations and civilizations, the easy seduction of manifest destiny and providence, and the wandering paths taken by Man in the search for freedom and progress, like the echoing paths of a sound in the darkness.

***[Author's Notes: The acoustic-wave technology described here is actually based on a real sensing technique, as disclosed by US Patent #4,644,100, "Surface Acoustic Wave Touch Panel System," invented by Michael C. Brenner and James J. Fitzgibbon, issued on February 17, 1987. The diagrams in this story are based on the drawings found in the patent.]***

# Voyage to a Distant Star

*C.S.E. Cooney*

*For Caitlyn Paxson*

**1. ABDUCTION**

Am I an afterthought?
A carcass for his quota?
Until he came for me, I thought
The Beast fastidious.

Of the miners, he amassed the tall and strong
Of their women, selected only from the loveliest
Those sinewy of limb and clean
The nimblest of the children, he snatched
The kindle-eyed, the quick of tongue
Plucked like flowers from the open pits
Drawn fast unto his breast, and brought
Into his hold, his silver hall
His tower in the stars.

And I—crook-backed and bent—
I who cooked for all the camp and none too well—
I too old to bear a child and never so inclined—
I am here,
Set down among the rest.

Outside,
The stars begin to move.
A drowsiness and lethargy has come upon me.

## 2. AWAKENING

All right, and so, the fight's not gone as planned.
A standoff.

Some of us are saying, "Let him free and set him
To his silver wheel, chain him, put a flame
Beneath his feet and make him guide us back, back
Through blackness and the hurtling stars,
Back home
Where we belong."

Our eyes deep fires in pared-down faces; I think we
Woke too soon.

My very bones feel different
As if, while we were sleeping
Each anchored in our crystal crèche
The Beast reshaped us
Carved us in his image, starting in our innards
Till slowly we began to mirror him
Who is no man.

My lungs burn.
Too new.
Oxygen, now, would drown me.

John says
(John talks big
Everything about John is big
His rugged frame, his ruddy beard
His rock-breaking hands, his baritone
Such thunder in this hollow, silver place)
John says to all us gathered:

*"There is no going back*
*There is us, there is this*
*There is forward and ahead."*

Are these words his, or were they put there?
John, I note, did not partake of our rebellion
He's been up here the longest, was the first
Perhaps he is a favorite of the Beast.

The Beast is in the brig
There hounded by three hundred miners and their kin
He's locked himself inside
And all our pickaxes won't dent that silver door.

But when John's Jenny
To wile the tedium of siege
Puts her quill to dulcimer
The Beast begins to slam himself
Against his prison walls.

He howls.
I think he's singing.

**3. SURVIVORS**

They call her Lionheart, that girl
The last one taken in the raids
They say it was her choice to come—
She bartered with the Beast
For a seat upon his silver ship
Begged and pleaded
Offered up her body as a swap.

Oh, they say many sly things
And shun her.

But I trust the sadness in her eyes
Bright anthracite, like the seams back home
And her hair's a thick pour of molasses
Like I'd use in my cornpones
And she misses her sister, and I miss my own
And to my sympathies, she makes confession.

"I hear the foul things they mutter
But how they are mistaken!
Ma soeur, she had a lover, and he loved her
They were promised to each other
And—but this must be our secret, friend—
She was to bear their child."

Her eyes reflect the silver of these walls
Her eyes, refashioned and refined
In those hundred months or years we slept
Naked and enshrined, alone each in our crèche
Under the Beast's eye and knife;
Her eyes can see in total darkness.

"I almost was too late—
Le Bête—he'd snatched ma soeur already!
Had frozen her in sleep
And too, the babe inside her womb!
No larger than a fingernail.

Of course he chose ma soeur
She is an angel.

I cried to him:
*Take me! Take me instead, sweet monseigneur!*

I lied to him
I said that she was sick
My sister
I told him it was cancer and the cough
I told him that the coal had crawled into her lungs
That her baby was a tumor who devoured her
I told him I was strong
I begged and hung about his neck
I kissed his metal scales.

He laughed—
Do you think that throbbing wail is laughter?—
And loosed her from his rimy sleep

Her rosiness crept in
The frost began to vanish from her face
She breathed.

And that was all I saw
Before he took me in his arms
And bore me nightward."

**4. APPROACH**

The Beast has passed beyond us.

Like a spider spits her silk
Like a worm spins its cocoon
His own secretions have entombed him
He sleeps inside his crystal crèche
We are alone.

Nor does his silver wheel budge for us.
It is course-stuck.

Jenny plays her dulcimer
The silver walls
Play back to her
A wondrous symphony.
But she cannot play us home
Her eyes are silver shutters, except those times
She looks at John.

John speaks of days to come
And soon
Tells tales of the world we are to work
As miners, like we were on Earth
Of creatures yet unknown to man
Who shall be known to us
Of excavation sites the size of cities
The fabled ore we'll find there

*This adventure*, Johnny says
*Will be our genesis story*
*Our seed of glory.*

John smiles and speaks, smiles and speaks
And speaks and speaks
First booming, then braying, then rasping
Lately he looks haggard
Like any mouthpiece so used
By his Lord.

The Lionheart listens
Though her mouth is grim
Others conspire in corners to be quit of him.

I wander far from them, and range abroad
Room to empty room
Silver wall to silver hall
Attempt to learn this ship that learned our Jenny's music
It is teaching her, in secret
A few songs of its own—
I'll never tell.
John is right.
There is us, there is here.
And in the distance how that distant star
Draws ever near.

My spine against the silver wall,
I turn from time to time
To scratch these words upon it.

Soon, I think
Before we land at last
These walls will start to scratch back.

# WereMoonMother

## *Brittany Warman*

All Sequence Start.

*ten*

The moon howls in my blood, a mother calling to her child.
My eyes are closed, the pregnant silence around me complete,
too still, mechanical.
I do not look at the others,
do not say a word in their tongue.
They would not understand, they do not hear you.
My human hands clench and I can feel
the familiar pulse of change beginning beneath my skin.
Outside, the summer sky glows blue and clear,
hiding my mother's full face to everyone but me.

*nine*

The years I have spent waiting for this last countdown
streak across my eyes like comets.
I have solved their mathematical puzzles,
endured their simulations, passed their tests,
studied and trained with the best they have to offer.
I have lit candles at your altar
and begged for forgiveness, mother, for understanding.
These scientists,
they do not know you.

*eight*

I have suffered their ignorance
and prepared my body/mind/soul to meet you, mother.

I have fought the wolf in me
in order to fit into a white suit,
to wear the flag of my human birth country on my breast,
and shoot myself into the skies.
Have you seen my work, mother?
Are you proud?

*seven*

How many times have I torn my eyes from you
to look at their books and their machines?
I have denied my wild heart behind steel-rimmed glasses,
become faint with the effort of hiding.
I have lied and lied for you,
craved the taste of senseless death and said no,
cried weak, man-made tears.

*six*

Full moon nights I spent sleepless in human beds
and willed my body to ignore your call.
I ripped through the veins in my wrists with my teeth
to distract my heart, to feel anything else
but your wounded presence in the darkness,
my desire for you burning me alive.

*ignition sequence start*

*three*

Your body under my paws—
a moment of perfection
before I dissolve into stars.

*two*

I hear the blast before I feel it,
wait for weightlessness.

*one*

I will connect our hearts, mother, as has never been done before.

Ignition.

# Delirious Mythology

## *About the Contributors*

**Liz Bourke** is a cranky person who reads books and occasionally writes poems. A 2014 Hugo Award nominee for best fan writer, she is presently reading for a PhD in Classics at Trinity College, Dublin.

**Lisa M. Bradley** resides in Iowa with her spouse, child, and two cats. Her short fiction and poetry have infiltrated *Goblin Fruit*, *Stone Telling*, *Strange Horizons*, *Cicada*, and other publications. She loves gothic country and Americana music, broken taboos, Spanglish, and horror films—evidence of which you'll find in her collection, *The Haunted Girl* (Aqueduct Press, Fall 2014).

**Marie Brennan** is an anthropologist and folklorist who shamelessly pillages her academic fields for material. She is currently misapplying her professors' hard work to the Victorian adventure series *The Memoirs of Lady Trent*. She is also the author of the Doppelanger duology of *Warrior* and *Witch*, the urban fantasy *Lies and Prophecy*, the Onyx Court historical fantasy series, and more than forty short stories.

**Georgina Bruce**'s stories have been published in *Interzone*, *Daily Science Fiction*, *Clockwork Phoenix 3: New Tales of Beauty and Strangeness*, and various other magazines and anthologies. She is currently writing a novel.

**Beth Cato**'s the author of *The Clockwork Dagger*, a steampunk fantasy novel from Harper Voyager. Her short fiction is in *InterGalactic Medicine Show*, *Beneath Ceaseless Skies*, and *Daily Science Fiction*. She's a Hanford, California native transplanted to the Arizona desert, where she lives with her husband, son, and requisite cat. Her website is BethCato.com.

**C.S.E. Cooney** is a Rhode Island writer, who lives across the street from a Victorian Strolling Park. She is the author of *How To Flirt in Faerieland and Other Wild Rhymes* and *Jack o' the Hills*. "Witch, Beast, Saint," the first of her erotic fairytales from *The Witch's Garden Series*, appeared in *Strange Horizons* in late July 2014, with the second in the series, "The Witch in the Almond Tree," available on Amazon as an ebook. With her fellow artists in the Banjo Apocalypse Crinoline Troubadours, Cooney appears at conventions and other venues, singing from their growing collection of "Distant Star Ballads," dramatizing fiction, and performing such story-poems as "The Sea King's Second Bride," for which she won the Rhysling Award in 2011. Her first short fiction collection, *Bone Swans and Other Stories,* is forthcoming from Mythic Delirium Books in 2015.

Last year, Elektrik Milk Bath Press published a collection of **Jennifer Crow**'s mythology and folklore poetry, called *The First Bite of the Apple*, now a nominee for the Suzette Haden Elgin Award. She lives with her family near a waterfall in western New York.

**Galen Dara** likes monsters, mystics, dead things and extremely ripe apricots. She has created art for 47 North Publishing, *Fireside Magazine, Lightpseed, Apex, Goblin Fruit, Lackington's Magazine*, and Edge Publishing. Her art is included in *Spectrum* 20 and 21. She won the 2011 Orycon33 Art Show Directors Choice Award, the 2013 Hugo Award for Best Fan Artist, and is a nominee for the 2013 Hugo Award for Professional Artist. When Galen is not working on a project you can find her on the edge of the Sonoran Desert, climbing mountains and hanging out with a loving assortment of human and animal companions. Her website is www.galendara.com and you can follow her on twitter @galendara.

**Robert Davies** writes weird fiction. His stories have appeared in *The Year's Best Dark Fantasy & Horror 2010*, *Weird Tales*, *Black Static*, *Interzone*, *Shroud Magazine*, and elsewhere. He lives in Somerville, Massachusetts, with his high school sweetheart Sara, two cats Lilith and Tiamat, and a lot of books. He is working on his first novel, *The Bitter Taste of the World Snake's Tail.*

**Amal El-Mohtar** is the Nebula-nominated author of *The Honey Month*, a collection of spontaneous short stories and poems written to the taste of twenty-eight different kinds of honey. She is a two-time winner of the Rhysling Award for Best Short Poem, and edits *Goblin Fruit*, an online quarterly dedicated to fantastical poetry. Her work has appeared in multiple venues online and in print, including *Apex*, *Strange Horizons*, *Stone Telling*, and *Glitter & Mayhem*, a speculative nightclub anthology. Find her online at amalelmohtar.com, and on Twitter as tithenai.

**Nicole Kornher-Stace** lives in New Paltz, NY. Her short fiction and poetry has appeared in a number of magazines and anthologies, including *Best American Fantasy*, *Clockwork Phoenix 3* and *4*, *The Mammoth Book of Steampunk*, *Apex*, and *Fantasy Magazine*. She is the author of *Desideria*, *Demon Lovers and Other Difficulties*, and *The Winter Triptych*. Her latest novel, *Archivist Wasp*, is forthcoming from Big Mouth House, Small Beer Press's YA imprint, in 2015. She can be found online at www.nicolekornherstace.com.

**Yoon Ha Lee**'s works have appeared in *Lightspeed*, *Tor.com*, *Beneath Ceaseless Skies*, and *The Magazine of Fantasy and Science Fiction*. Her collection *Conservation of Shadows* came out in 2013 from Prime Books. Currently she lives in Louisiana with her family and has not yet been eaten by gators.

**Sandi Leibowitz** is a native New Yorker, school librarian, classical singer and writer of speculative poetry and fiction. Her works have appeared in *Apex*, *Strange Horizons*, *Stone Telling*, *Goblin Fruit*, *Luna Station Quarterly*, *Metastasis*, and Ellen Datlow's *Best Horror of the Year 5*, and other publications. She lives in a leafy aerie with two ghost-dogs and the occasional dragon, but you may visit her at www.sandileibowitz.com.

**Ken Liu** (http://kenliu.name) is an author and translator of speculative fiction, as well as a lawyer and programmer. A winner of the Nebula, Hugo, and World Fantasy Awards, he has been published in *The Magazine of Fantasy & Science Fiction*, *Asimov's*, *Analog*, *Clarkesworld*, *Lightspeed*, and *Strange Horizons*, among other places. He lives with his family near Boston, Massachusetts.

Ken's debut novel, *The Grace of Kings*, the first in a silkpunk epic fantasy series, will be published by Saga Press, Simon & Schuster's new genre fiction imprint, in April 2015. Saga will also publish a collection of his short stories.

**Brigitte McCray**'s poems, short stories, and essays have also appeared in *Southern Humanities Review*, *storysouth.com*, *Red Rock Review*, *Timber Creek Review*, *The Journal of Homosexuality*, *Ecozon@*, and *The Explicator*. She's at work on Southern fantastic poems and short stories. Originally from Southern Appalachia, Brigitte currently teaches writing and literature in the Midwest.

**Lynette Mejía** writes science fiction, fantasy, and horror prose and poetry. Her work has appeared or is forthcoming in *Goblin Fruit*, *Dreams & Nightmares*, *Strange Horizons*, *Ideomancer*, and *Star*Line*. She is currently working on a master's degree in English Literature at the University of Louisiana-Lafayette, and lives in Carencro, Louisiana, with her husband, three children, six cats, and one dog. You can find her online at www.lynettemejia.com.

**Virginia M. Mohlere** was born on one solstice, and her sister was born on the other. Her chronic writing disorder stems from early childhood. She lives in the swamps of Houston and writes with a fountain pen that is extinct in the wild. Her work has been seen in *Cabinet des Fées*, *Jabberwocky*, *Lakeside Circus*, *Goblin Fruit*, *Strange Horizons*, and *MungBeing*.

**Karthika Naïr** was born in India, lives in Paris, and works as a dance producer and curator. She is the author of *Bearings* (HarperCollins India, 2009), a poetry collection; *DESH: Memories inherited, borrowed, invented* (MC2 Grenoble, 2013), a dance diary; and *Le Tigre de Miel/ The Honey Hunter* (Editions Hélium, France/ Zubaan Books, India, 2013), a children's book illustrated by Joëlle Jolivet. She was the principal story-and-scriptwriter of DESH (2011), choreographer Akram Khan's multiple-award-winning dance production. She is currently working on her next poetry collection, *Until the Lions*, a retelling of the Mahabharata war in eighteen voices.

**Mari Ness** is the author of *Through Immortal Shadows Singing*, an experimental novella-in-poetry. She has also published poetry and short fiction in multiple publications, including *Strange Horizons*, *Goblin Fruit*, *Clarkesworld*, *Apex Magazine*, and Tor.com. For a longer list of her works, check out her official blog at marikness.wordpress.com, and to keep up with what she's doing, follow her on Twitter at @mari_ness. She lives in central Florida.

**Yukimi Ogawa** lives in a small town in Tokyo where she writes in English but never speaks the language. She still wonders why it works that way. Her fiction can be found in such places as *Strange Horizons* and *Clockwork Phoenix 4*.

**Rhonda Parrish** is driven by a desire to do All The Things. She has been the publisher and editor-in-chief of *Niteblade Magazine* for over five years now (which is like 25 years in Internet time) and is the editor of the forthcoming World Weaver Press anthology, *Fae*.

In addition, Rhonda is a writer whose work has been included or is forthcoming in dozens of publications, including *Tesseracts 17: Speculating Canada from Coast to Coast* and *Imaginarium 2012: The Best Canadian Speculative Writing*.

Her website, updated weekly, is at http://www.rhondaparrish.com.

**S. Brackett Robertson** is often found up a tree. Her work has previously appeared in *Goblin Fruit*, *Mythic Delirium*, and *Inkscrawl*. She frequents museums and would like to visit more ancient cities.

**J.C. Runolfson**'s work has appeared in *Goblin Fruit*, *Stone Telling*, and *Strange Horizons*, among others. She likes to wreak havoc with fairy tales in addition to wildly speculating about historical personages whose claims to fame tend toward the weird and uncanny. Like her beloved shelties, she has a bad habit of chewing her toys to pieces.

**Cedar Sanderson** is a writer, blogger, and businesswoman who can be found in her office pounding the keyboard when she isn't at school studying to be a Mad Scientist. Her work has been published by Stonycroft Publishing, Naked Reader Press, and *Something*

*Wicked*. She is the author of the young adult novel *Vulcan's Kittens*, and her contemporary fantasy series that began with *Pixie Noir* will continue with *Trickster Noir*, scheduled to be released in May 2014. She writes regular blog columns at *Amazing Stories Magazine* and the *Mad Genius Club*, in addition to her own writing blog, www.cedarwrites.com. She prefers science fiction, mostly writes fantasy, and dabbles in nonfiction when her passion is stirred.

Nebula nominee and Sturgeon finalist **Kenneth Schneyer** composed exam questions for over twenty years as a professor of humanities and legal studies. His stories appear in Mike Allen's *Clockwork Phoenix 3* and *Clockwork Phoenix 4*, as well as in *Analog, Strange Horizons, Beneath Ceaseless Skies, Daily Science Fiction, Escape Pod, Podcastle*, and various hypothetical problems. Stillpoint Digital Press released his first collection, *The Law & the Heart*, in 2014. He's a graduate of the Clarion Writers Workshop and a member of both Codex Writers and the Cambridge Science Fiction Workshop. He lives in Rhode Island with three champion test takers and a cat who defies paradox. Look him up on Facebook, on Twitter, and at ken-schneyer.livejournal.com.

**Alexandra Seidel** probably caught the myth and fairy tale bug while she was out in the woods one midsummer day. Meanwhile, the disease has turned her into a poet, writer, and editor. Her work may be found in *Strange Horizons, Goblin Fruit, Stone Telling*, and elsewhere. You can follow her on Twitter (@Alexa_Seidel) or read her blog: www.tigerinthematchstickbox.blogspot.com.

**David Sklar** grew up in Michigan, where the Michipeshu nibbled his toes when Lake Superior was feeling frisky. His published works include he anthology *Trafficking in Magic, Magicking in Traffic*, coedited with Sarah Avery (Tales from Rugosa Coven), as well as fiction and poetry in *Strange Horizions, Ladybug, Nightmare Magazine*, and other places. David lives with his wife, their two barbarians, and a secondhand familiar, all of whom he almost supports as a freelance writer and editor. Over his life so far, he has eaten kangaroo meat, posed naked for a Tarot deck, pitched a sitcom to NBC, and had his shoelace bitten in half by a rabbit.

For more about David and his work, please visit http://david-writing.com.

**Christina Sng** is a poet, writer, and occasional toymaker. Her poetry has received several Honorable Mentions in *The Year's Best Fantasy and Horror* as well as two Rhysling nominations. She lives with her family and their enigmatic cat north of the Equator.

**Sonya Taaffe**'s short fiction and poetry can be found in the collections *Postcards from the Province of Hyphens* (Prime Books), *Singing Innocence and Experience* (Prime Books), and *A Mayse-Bikhl* (Papaveria Press), and in anthologies including *Beyond Binary: Genderqueer and Sexually Fluid Speculative Fiction*, *The Moment of Change: An Anthology of Feminist Speculative Poetry*, *People of the Book: A Decade of Jewish Science Fiction & Fantasy*, *The Year's Best Fantasy and Horror*, *The Alchemy of Stars: Rhysling Award Winners Showcase*, and *The Best of Not One of Us*. She is currently senior poetry editor at *Strange Horizons*; she holds master's degrees in Classics from Brandeis and Yale and once named a Kuiper belt object. She lives in Somerville with her husband and their two cats.

**Patty Templeton** is roughly 25 apples tall and 11,000 coffee cups into her life. She wears red sequins and stomping boots while writing, then hits up back-alley dance bars and honky tonks. Her stories are full of ghosts, freaks, fools, underdogs, blue collar heroes, and never giving up, even when life is giving you shit. She has appeared in *Pseudopod*, *Podcastle*, *Steam Powered II*, and *Criminal Class Review*. She won the first-ever Naked Girls Reading Literary Honors Award and has been a runner-up for the Mary Wollstonecraft Shelley Award. Her first novel, *There Is No Lovely End*, debuted this summer. For more info, head over to PattyTempleton.com.

**Brittany Warman** is a PhD student in English and Folklore at The Ohio State University, where she concentrates on the intersection between literature and folklore, particularly fairy tale retellings. Her creative work has been published by or is forthcoming from *Jabberwocky Magazine*, *Ideomancer*, *inkscrawl*, *Cabinet des Fees: Scheherezade's Bequest*, and others. She can be found online at brittanywarman.com.

**Jane Yolen**, often called "the Hans Christian Andersen of America," is the author of over 350 published books, including *Owl Moon, The Devil's Arithmetic,* and *How Do Dinosaurs Say Goodnight?* The books range from rhymed picture books and baby board books, through middle grade fiction, poetry collections, nonfiction, and up to novels and story collections for young adults and adults. She has won two Nebulas, a World Fantasy Grand Master Award, and been named a Grand Master of sf/fantasy poetry by the Science Fiction Poetry Association. Six colleges and universities have given her honorary doctorates, and her Skylark Award—given by NESFA (the New England Science Fiction Association)—set her good coat on fire.

On weekdays, **Mike Allen** writes the arts column for the daily newspaper in Roanoke, Va. Most of the rest of his time he devotes to writing, editing, and publishing. His first novel, a dark fantasy called *The Black Fire Concerto,* appeared in 2013, and he's written a sequel, *The Ghoulmaker's Aria*, that's in the revision stage. He edits and publishes the Clockwork Phoenix anthologies and the digital magazine *Mythic Delirium.* Antinatter Press will premiere his first collection of short fiction, *Unseaming*, at the 2014 World Fantasy Connvention.

He receives a ton of help with all this editing from his wife, artist and horticulturalist **Anita Allen**. Her paintings and assemblages have appeared in juried art shows and on the covers of past issues of *Mythic Delirium.*

Their pets, Loki (canine) and Persephone and Pandora (feline) provide distractions. You can follow Mike's exploits as a writer at descentintolight.com, as an editor at mythicdelirium.com, and all at once on Twitter at @mythicdelirium.

## Copyright Notices

CPSIA information can be obtained at www.ICGtesting.com
Printed in the USA
LVOW12s1733211014

409812LV00006B/751/P